BORN HEARTLESS 4

T.J. Edwards

Lock Down Publications and Ca$h
Presents
BORN HEARTLESS 4
A Novel by *T.J. Edwards*

T.J. Edwards

Lock Down Publications
P.O. Box 944
Stockbridge, Ga 30281

Lock Down Publications
Like our page on Facebook: Lock Down Publications @ www.facebook.com/lockdownpublications.ldp
Cover design and layout by: **Dynasty Cover Me**
Book interior design by: **Shawn Walker**
Edited by: **Jill Alicea**

Stay Connected with Us!

Text **LOCKDOWN** to 22828 to stay up-to-date with new releases, sneak peaks, contests and more…

Thank you!

Submission Guideline.

Submit the first three chapters of your completed manuscript to ldpsubmissions@gmail.com, subject line: Your book's title. The manuscript must be in a .doc file and sent as an attachment. Document should be in Times New Roman, double spaced and in size 12 font. Also, provide your synopsis and full contact information. If sending multiple submissions, they must each be in a separate email.

Have a story but no way to send it electronically? You can still submit to LDP/Ca$h Presents. Send in the first three chapters, written or typed, of your completed manuscript to:

LDP: Submissions Dept
P.O. Box 944
Stockbridge, Ga 30281

DO NOT send original manuscript. Must be a duplicate.

Provide your synopsis and a cover letter containing your full contact information.

Thanks for considering LDP and Ca$h Presents.

Dedications

This book is dedicated to my amazingly, beautiful stomp down wife, Mrs. Jelissa Shante Edwards, who knows firsthand what this Ski Mask life is all about.

I've had to feed our family many nights using that to make it happen. But, for you, I had to find another way because you deserve the best, and my place to be is beside you, protecting you at all times.

You're my motivating force that keeps me going. No matter how old you get, you'll always be my baby girl. So, deal with it. I love you forever and always.

Your husband.

R.I.P to my beautiful mother, Deborah L. Edwards

Shout out to Cash and Shawn. I love y'all with all my heart...not only as a C.E.O and C.O.O, but as brother and sister. This is me and my wife's home. You already know that our loyalty is sealed in blood. Mad love to the entire LDP family.

Also to my supportive reader, Claudia Calaway-Burrell, thank you so much for your continued support. My wife and I truly appreciate you, Queen. God bless.

T.J. Edwards

Chapter 1

"You gotta excuse me for being late, TJ. I had another more serious matter that I had to tend to," Juelz said when he pulled up on me rolling a black Jaguar four nights later. The windows were tinted pitch black. He had a black bandana around his neck. I could tell that he was ready to ride on a nigga.

I got into the Jaguar and slammed the door. "It's all good. What's the business though?"

"That fool Jay tripping. I had to turn down a move out there in Phoenix that he wanted me to handle. Now he got his panties all in a bunch and shit. You know how that shit goes when a ma'fucka so used to you saying yes that when you finally say no, they start acting all funny and shit." He pulled off.

"Yeah. But fuck, dude, what's up with Deion? Where is he supposed to be at?" I asked, cutting straight to the chase.

"That nigga fuckin' around over there in Motown. He got a few that's honoring him like he's a prince or something."

"Word?"

Juelz nodded. "I hear he fuckin' with that heroin now too. Tough."

"It was only a matter of time. He grew up with my pops being his role model. You should've already known where that was going to get him."

"Yeah, well, hopefully we'll be able to handle that nigga. Then we won't have to worry about his ass no more. I feel like we've been chasing behind what happened to Marie for a million years."

I nodded. "Well, let's go end this shit. I'm ready to get on with my life, too."

"It ain't that simple though. You see, Deion is a major nigga in the game now. He's moving a lot of weight, and since he is, he's been really useful to the cartel. You already know how they get down."

"Nigga, so what is you saying?" I was getting irritated.

"I'm saying, if we hit this nigga, we finna have some serious consequences to deal with because it will be an unsanctioned hit. The cartel frowns upon that, especially if it messes with their money flow."

"Yo, so you saying that this nigga get a pass for what he did to my little sister? Are you fuckin' kidding me?" I snapped, ready to punch Juelz in his jaw.

Juelz shook his head. "Nigga, chill. I ain't saying that. You already know ain't no hoe in me. I'm asking you if you think it'll be worth going to war over. And I ain't just talking about no regular war either. I'm talking some all-out serious heat from them ma'fuckin' killas down south. You think it's worth it?"

"You muthafuckin' right." I didn't give a fuck who I had to go up against. Deion had to pay for what he'd done to Marie. There was no way around that. If that meant that a ma'fucka was gon' kill me right after I killed him, then so be it. That vengeance shit ran cold in my blood.

"A'ight then. We gotta do what we gotta do then." He got to texting on his phone after he pulled up to a stop sign. It took him a few minutes to write it, then he pulled back off. "Shorty, you already know that I'm rolling with you until the wheels fall off."

"I know that. Let's handle this last bit of business and be done wit' it."

Juelz's phone buzzed again. He read the message and frowned. "Dawg, I gotta go holler at Jay real quick."

"Man, fuck Jay. We gotta knock off Deion."

Juelz shook his head. "This shit serious, nigga. I gotta go holler at dude whether I want to or not." He looked sick.

"Fuck you mean?"

"It's just one of those things, TJ. Let me handle this right quick and we'll go twist that nigga cap back in a minute. That's my word."

"Yeah, nigga, whatever. Let's just go."

***

Jay was a big-ass white boy that stood at 5'10". He was bald with a reddish-gray beard and menacing hazel eyes. He had tattoos all over his neck and arms. He was Juelz's direct plug from Chicago to the cartels south of the border. It was because of him that Juelz had been able to come up so quickly in the game.

Juelz pulled into the garage of Jay's auto repair shop. Jay stood in the middle of the floor, almost daring Juelz to hit him as he pulled in. I was so irritated that had I been the one driving, I might have. After Juelz pulled into the garage, the door was lowered. Jay's men came out of the shadows with assault rifles in their hands, aiming them at the car.

"Juelz, what the fuck is this?" I snapped, looking over to him.

"Nigga, be smooth. This nigga just acting like a bitch right now. Whatever you do, don't help me. It's just a process. Trust me." He lowered the window and stuck his hands out of it. "Yo, Jay, call off your dogs."

Jay walked over to the car with a mug on his face. He yanked the door open and pulled Juelz out of it. "You no-good muthafucker. You think you can say no to me after I made your ass?" He threw him to the ground and kicked him in the stomach.

I placed my hand on the handle of my gun. I was ready to go for what I knew. Fuck Juelz's orders for me not to help him. How could I not when this big-ass white dude was treating him that way?

He yanked Juelz up and slammed him to the wall, upped a Glock .9, and stuffed it in his mouth. "You wanna tell me no now, boy? Huh?"

Juelz closed his eyes. I could see his chest heaving. His hands balled into fists off and on. A thick vein appeared in his neck.

"Aw, you're tough, right? You got a few murders under your belt and you think you're tough now? Huh? You project filth! You don't ever say no to me. You're done." He spat in his face and threw him to the ground again. He cocked his pistol and aimed it down at Juelz. He took one step back and fired his gun repeatedly.

"Noooooo!" I heard myself hollering as I ran toward them with both guns in my hands.

Before I could make it to them, the garage door raised and I saw a bunch of flashlights and police suited in SWAT gear with assault rifles in their hands.

"Freeze! Freeze! Freeze! Police! Get down on the ground! Now!"

The shock of seeing so many police in one place at one time seemed to make my knees weak. I buckled and fell face first onto the concrete of the auto repair shop. When I hit the floor, I stuffed both pistols into my waistband. *Fuck! How did this happen?* I was finna go back to prison. I started to imagine the inside of a prison cell at the same time my son flashed into my mind. I hadn't even gotten the chance to get to know him the way that I should have. I thought about Punkin. I should have been more respectful to her. I should have taken her more seriously. Now it was too late.

What would have become of me and Jelissa? How much time would they give me in prison? Did they know about all of the bodies? All of these thoughts went through my head as I stayed on my stomach, trying to figure out what would be the smartest move to make in this moment.

Jay and his crew of white savages fell to the ground with their hands over their heads. The police rushed them with black helmets on their heads and fell beside them with their service weapons to their heads. Jay cursed out loud and slung spit from his mouth across the room. "You set me up, Juelz. You muthafucka! I should have killed your nigger ass!"

More and more police ran into the room. I reluctantly glanced over to where Juelz was laying down and expected to see a puddle of blood. I didn't want to see my right hand man slain like that, but I had to see him one last time before I was hauled away to prison. Juelz had been the only real brother that I had ever known. His death would shatter me. Jay continued to holler his obscenities as I mugged him. His men looked sick as people with pneumonia. They were handcuffed and shackled. Jay kept snapping.

When I turned back to see Juelz for the last time, a strong chill went down my spine. Juelz climbed to a push-up position and stood up. He had a big smile on his face. He dusted himself off and pulled his .45 from his back. He walked over to Jay and looked down on him. "Yeah, bitch, you can't outthink me."

Jay looked up to him as if he had seen a ghost. His eyes were bucked. He turned a bright shade of pink. "You son of a bitch! Let me out of these cuffs right now! You answer to me!"

"Nawl, ma'fucka, not no more I don't." Juelz knelt beside him and slammed his .45 to his temple. "What's the combination to that big trunk in the back? Huh?"

"Fuck you. I ain't giving you shit!" Jay yelled.

"Aww, po' baby, you mad 'cause you got out thought by a boy from the hood? Huh?" He forced the gun harder into his temple. "The combination." Blood began to form around the barrel.

"Argh! Okay! Okay! It's the address to this place. But you're making a big mistake. The product belongs to the Dark Knight's Cartel. If you rip them off, they are going to destroy you. You know how all of this works."

"Fuck them!" Juelz gave a signal and one of the police officers took his helmet off. I saw that he was nothing more than one of the li'l homies from the hood. He had a red bandana around the lower portion of his face. "Yo, the combo is three, forty-seven, eighty-five. Go check and make sure that shit is valid. TJ, what the fuck you still down on the ground for? Get yo' ass up and go make sure that this is the right combination with the li'l homie."

I stood up, still in shock. I was happy that they weren't the real police. I wasn't trying to do any more prison time for anybody. I was also thankful that Juelz was still alive, yet pissed that he would set all of this shit up without letting me know what the business was.

I rushed to catch up with Juelz's worker. When I got into the office, he was punching in the last sequence of numbers into the massive safe. He finished and stepped back. The safe clicked loudly and opened with a sizzling sound. He pulled it open. I saw two rows of aluminum foil-wrapped heroin packaged with pictures of a blue donkey on them. Directly below them were clear packages of white powder. These bricks had the picture of a red donkey on them. Altogether, it looked like three hundred kilos.

"Yo shorty, dis ma'fucka open and I'm seeing everything that I am supposed to. Now what?"

Before he finished all of his words, the room was flooded with police officers that had duffel bags. They rushed into the room and began to stuff the bags with kilo after kilo.

I left out of there and went back into the repair shop where they worked on the cars. Juelz was standing over Jay with a Draco in his hand. He had the long barrel of the gun pressed to his left eyelid. "This how dat shit looks when you underestimate a ma'fucka just because of my skin color and where I'm from. Rest in hell, you bitch-ass pussy." He squeezed the trigger and splattered Jay all over the concrete.

Bullet shells jumped out of the assault rifle and rolled across the concrete with smoke coming from them. Juelz stepped on Jay's torso, showing the ultimate disrespect, and walked around the room offing the rest of the men that were with Jay. When he finished, his men ran past him and loaded up all of the duffel bags into the vehicles that were waiting outside.

He placed his arm around my shoulder. "Dis hit finna make us dope kings, nigga. We are about to take over Chicago. Never doubt me, TJ. I got us. Let's go!" he hollered.

Chapter 2

It was two months after we hit the lick on Jay, and I was seeing more money that I ever had in all of my life. Juelz gave me a hundred kilos to work with. He gave me fifty in coke and fifty in pure heroin.

I sat back in the trap with two of Chicago's finest chefs and we stepped on each brick just before I flooded the entire north side of the city. I had fifteen units that I hit up daily either to drop off a pack or to pick up the cash that was owed to me.

The operations were running smoothly and the money was coming so fast that it spooked me. Instead of Juelz snatching up a few members of Twelve to put on the payroll, he found a way to buy out an entire precinct that operated in our district. We had diplomatic immunity in our slums, and that made me feel invincible. While I knew that things like this could only last for a short amount of time, I couldn't help but to become spoiled by the moment.

Punkin started to apply the pressure worse than ever after seeing how deep I was becoming in the game. A few months after me and Juelz's major lick, I pulled up in front of her house in a good Bentley truck sitting on thirty-two-inch throwback Sprewells. I'd always had a thing for rims, and that didn't stop even when my shit wasn't moving. I had to plush out my Bentley truck the same way.

Punkin was coming out of the house with Junior in a carrier when I pulled up and beeped the horn. She was trying to juggle the carrier in one hand and the stroller in the other. I felt bogus as hell.

She stopped on the third stair and lowered her eyes to see who it was blowing their horn at her. It was mid-summer, every bit of ninety plus degrees outside, with very little wind.

Punkin must have seen that it was me because she rolled her eyes and continued to come down the steps.

I hurried to her and caught her just before she came off of the last step. "Yo, you must still be feeling a way or something?" I took my son out of her arms.

She picked up the stroller and carried it down to the sidewalk. She opened it and motioned for me to give him to her. "TJ, what are you doing here? I thought you weren't messing with me no more." She kept her hands open, ready to receive Junior.

I kissed all over his fat cheeks. "I never said that. How could I ever be done messing with you when we have a son together? That doesn't make any sense." I lowered him into the stroller and strapped him in. She had him dressed in a blue and white Polo 'fit that I'd bought him a few weeks prior. He was even rocking the matching LeBron's. He looked dope.

"You ain't gotta say the words. The fact that you are still in those streets means that you are choosing them over us. I done heard some stories about you that leave me terrified." She took a hold of the handles of the stroller, fixed the part that was there to bring our son shade, and then kissed his chubby cheeks before walking down the street rolling him.

I walked beside her with the sun reflecting off of my gold Patek watch and Chanel glasses that transitioned to mirror tint when the sun hit them. "Where the fuck you finna go anyway?"

"That ain't yo' business, and I would appreciate it if you didn't use that language around our child. I don't want him hearing such negativity."

"That's my seed. That negative shit is in his soul already. Besides, he's one, he doesn't know the difference between good or bad words." She was always tripping about something.

"He's ten months, and it doesn't matter if you think he is able to understand the difference between good and bad words. I don't want you speaking them around him, and it is as simple as that." She kept rolling on her stuck-up shit.

"Punkin, I don't like how you talk to me when it comes to my son. You make it seem like I'm just this unfit dude that shouldn't have any part of his kid's life. That's foul because I stay flooding yo' ass wit' chips, and I do all that I can for him whenever you call me."

"I shouldn't have to call you when it comes to him. You should already be with us. And the fact that you think money can fill in the blanks of your absence is sad. Your son isn't old enough to understand the concept of money, but he does understand when Daddy is not there. You spend all of that time hustling in the streets. Who are you doing it for?"

"Y'all. That was a stupid-ass question." I felt myself becoming upset.

"I don't need your dirty money. I am well off. I have multiple properties that are doing quite well. I am very knowledgeable of the stock market, and as we speak, I am closing deals for two apartment buildings in Milwaukee. That is going to leave me way ahead. I am independent. Always have been, always will be. I don't need to lean on you for anything financial, and neither does your son. What we need is your presence. So miss me with that you 'trapping for us' talk. That fascinates those project broads, not a true woman that is about her own business." She crossed the street, pushing the stroller.

I looked both ways to make sure that no cars were coming. I couldn't tell how far Punkin was ready to go with Junior, so I ran back to my truck and grabbed my .9 millimeter.

Me and Juelz had beef with so many niggas in Chicago because we were cornering the market that I had to keep a gun on me all times. If I ever got caught without one, I was sure the enemy was going to take me out of the. When I got back to Punkin, she was singing the "Wheels on the Bus" song to Junior. I neglected to join in. "Where are you going, Shakia?"

"Aw, so now you're using my real name?" she asked dryly.

"Only when I get irritated wit' yo' ass. Now where the fuck are you going?" I grabbed her wrist.

"Language, boy." She looked down at Junior, then yanked her wrist away from me.

I released her. "Yo, just tell me what's up? You already know how I'm beefing with all of these bum-ass niggas in the city. I need to know where we are going and how long we are about to be there?"

Two black Suburbans pulled up with my shooters inside of them.

Punkin stopped and crossed her arms in front of her chest. "Ain't they for you?"

"Yeah, I need to let them know where we are going." I held up a finger to them.

Punkin's hair blew in the wind. She pulled a strand from her lips. "Damn, TJ, me and your son were about to go down to the beach and chill. I wanna finish this *A Love Worth the Wait* book that I am almost done reading before I have to go back to work tomorrow. I just wanted today to be a peaceful and serene day. Why are you trying to ruin it?"

"I just wanna be with my family. Is that too much to ask?"

"And them?" She pointed to the two truckloads of shooters.

"They are at work right now. Even when Barack was the president, everywhere he went he had Secret Servicemen tag along for the ride to make sure that he and his family got from point A to point B safe and sound. How long are we going to be at this beach?"

She sighed. "Damn, you just can't take a hint can you?"

I stepped into her face. "Hell ma'fuckin' nawl. The length of time, please?"

Instead of answering me, she pushed the stroller away and headed toward the beach that was only three blocks from her house. I told the shooters to stay close and to remain vigilant. Punkin was acting real foul toward me and I didn't like it. All I wanted was for me and her to come to an understanding when it came to our family.

Though the recent traumatic scene had been staged by Juelz, I still found myself wondering, what if it were for real? I didn't want to lose my son without ever getting the proper chance to get to know him, and deep down I knew that Punkin was really a good woman. I owed it to Junior to try to build something with his mother. That way I could have the family that I was never able to have. So as much as I wanted to turn around and say fuck her because of her disrespectful attitude, I caught up with her and tucked my pride aside.

"Look, Punkin, I know that we aren't on the best of terms right now, but I wanna take this day and get there. I don't wanna lose my son, and I don't wanna lose you. I understand that the two of you are a package deal, so how do we get this thing to work out for the greater good of our family?"

Punkin kept pushing him for a moment. Then she looked up to me. "You really wanna know how we get things to work out for the greater good?" She said this as if she had a slick comment to make.

"Yeah, tell me. Anything you say, I'll try my damndest to do."

"TJ, it's the same thing I've been saying to you. You need to leave those streets alone. If you can't leave them alone, then you have no place with either your son or myself."

"It's like that?" I frowned, feeling my blood run hot.

"It's just like that." She shook her head and kept rolling.

Instead of following her, I stopped and watched her get further and further away until she was at the beach. Once there, she looked back over her shoulder at me and shook her head again.

As much as I loved my son, I could no longer be in his mother's presence. She had a way of making me feel like a deadbeat even though I was doing all I could as a father.

Chapter 3

I was still feeling empty the next day when I pulled up at Jelissa's duplex. It was nine o'clock in the morning. I don't know why I had the audacity to just show up on her doorstep after not speaking to her for a few weeks, but I did. I made sure I was fresh from head to toe, fitted in Dolcé and Gabbana. I'd already come up with the plan of getting her to retwist my dreads for me if worse came to worst and I needed an excuse for popping up. I felt a li'l awkward ringing her doorbell. Punkin had me feeling so rejected that I was sure Jelissa was going to act the same way toward me. I braced myself and stood firm.

Jelissa pulled back the curtain of her front window and looked me up and down with a confused expression on her face. She had a scarf on her head. She pulled the curtain back into place and disappeared. When she opened the door, her curls were dropped and full of sheen. "TJ, what brings you here this early in the morning?"

"What, you got company of somethin'?"

"Nawl, it ain't that. It's just unexpected to see you is all." She stood looking up at me, confused.

"So can I come in or what?" I laughed shortly to mask the feeling of uncertainty inside of myself.

"Aw yeah, of course. Come on in." She turned to walk inside of the house.

My eyes trailed right down to that fat-ass booty that she had. She had a jiggle in her cheeks like no other female.

"I ain't mean to be popping up on you, but I need to talk. I've been going through a lot of shit with my baby mother." I closed the door and stepped into the room. I froze in place when I saw her three-year-old son, Rae'Jon, standing in the middle of the living with an iPad in his hand.

"Oooh, you said a bad word." He pointed at me.

"My fault, li'l homie. That was an accident. Here." I pulled out a knot of hundreds and gave him one.

He looked down at the money and smiled at me. "Thank you. But you still said a bad word."

"Rae'Jon, go into your room for a minute and let me talk to TJ," Jelissa ordered, leading him toward where I guessed his room would be.

"Okay, Mama." He waved goodbye to me and kept walking.

Jelissa came back into the living room minutes later with a look of exhaustion written across her face. She sat down on the couch across from me. "Sorry about that. That boy is getting too old too fast."

"Nawl, that's my fault. I gotta control my tongue better."

"The Bible says that men have been able to tame wild beasts of the Earth since the beginning of time, but that no man has ever been able to tame his own tongue. It's a hard task, but you can master it if you try hard enough. Not fully, according to the Word, but good enough." She laughed. "Can I get you somethin' to drink?" Her dimples popped on her caramel cheeks. Her brown eyes seemed to shine. She smelled like Cherry Blossoms.

I scooted to the edge of the couch. "Jelissa, I missed you."

She was silent for a moment. "I was not expecting you to say that."

"Yeah, well, it's the truth. I've been thinking about you real hard for months now. Why is it that every time I try and get up with you, you brush me off? What did I do to you?"

She sighed and ran her fingers through her hair. "You haven't done anything to me. I've simply had a lot going on and I'm already good where I am in my life. I am not in a

24

position to be with any man. I need to focus on myself and my child right now."

"I get that, but I still miss you like a ma'fucka. I ain't never yearned for no female before. All of this shit is new to me. Look, I don't know what I am supposed to do. You finna have to tell me." I hated feeling so damn vulnerable. I felt like I needed to kill a nigga or somethin' just to get that savage shit flowing back through my veins real tough.

"How are you missing me, TJ? We have only spent time together a few times. You missing me doesn't make sense."

"What, you think I'm lying or somethin'? What would I gain from that?"

She shrugged her shoulders. "I don't know. I guess I can admit that I have missed you in a sense as well. Every time we get together, I enjoy your company. You're a good person, regardless of what the streets of Chicago are saying about you."

"What are they saying?" I needed to know this. That way I could get an understanding as to how it was always so easy for her to blow me off as if I was a nobody-ass nigga and not a street king on my way to a million dollars in dirty money.

"They say that you are a cold-hearted murderer. A bully. A bloody drug lord. They call you a womanizer and a mob boss, everything except a child of God, that's for sure."

I lowered my head. "I'm a product of Chicago. They don't let niggas like me breathe in this city unless I am a bloody predator. I gotta keep my foot on the Game's neck. If I let up for one second, then I become prey and somebody gon' treat me like an antelope. Fuck that. Chicago is a jungle and I'm a lion. Fuck what the streets got to say because they only belong to the true killas." I leaned across the table and took her hands. "I am who they say I am, but there is also another side to me and I am trying so desperately to show him to you. I'm tired of all of the killing. The warring. The watching over my shoulder. My heart is black, Jelissa. I'm at the point where I need that love shit that everybody is talking about. I never felt it before and I need it before I go crazy.

"So what do you need me to do?" She looked into my eyes with her almond-shaped ones. She appeared so delicate, so small, yet so damn fine. I suddenly felt possessive over her and I couldn't understand why.

"I need you to teach me how to love. Please. I need you to go there with me." With all of the killing, drug dealing, plotting and scheming, and the fucking of multiple nobody-ass women, I was tired. I wanted something deeper. The streets were wearing me out and I was man enough to admit that. I needed a change of pace. I needed to find my place of refuge. Punkin for some reason didn't seem right to me, but Jelissa made my black heart call out to her in a way that I never thought was possible.

Jelissa lowered her head. "TJ, you ain't the only one that doesn't know how to love. As long as I've been alive, the only person I felt has ever loved me is my child. I don't know what it feels like to love a spouse or a boyfriend. That's why all of my love and time goes to Jesus. He promises to never leave or forsake me, and I believe Him."

"Damn, Jelissa, I don't know anything about that religious shit. Jehovah ain't finna accept me after all of the shit I've done. I've been whacking ma'fuckas left and right ever since I was a li'l nigga. He ain't about to listen to my prayers. Yo, I need you. Why can't you love me, or at the very least teach me how to love you the right way?"

She stood up and stepped to the window of her living room. She pulled back the curtain. "TJ, when you are as broken as I am, there is no way I could ever lead you in the right direction. My heart has been broken one time too many.

26

Now I find myself content with living for Jehovah and my child. I don't even think about me anymore. I'm a lost cause."

I got up and eased behind her with my eyes closed. My arms circled her waist and pulled her back to me. She felt so small, so slender, so perfect. Her booty was pudgy in my lap. I inhaled her scent and groaned. "If you're lost, then let me find you, shorty. Let me find in you what I have never been able to find in myself or anybody else."

"And what is that?" She leaned back into me, placing her hands over mine, which were already around her waist.

"A reason to love and live." I kissed the top of her head. "You've always felt so perfect in my arms. I hate letting you go sometimes." It was the truth.

She turned around and slid her arms around my neck. She looked up into my eyes. "Why do you want me so bad? Don't you know I am damaged goods?"

"All I see is a diamond. I wanna cherish you, and I wanna leave this pain behind through you. I swear to God all I need is the chance to do you right. I won't trick you off. You got my word on that." I kissed her forehead and rested my lips on her skin. It felt hot.

"I got so much to accomplish. I need to be able to build a future for my son. His father is a dead beat. He doesn't help me do nothing, yet he is still dragging me back and forth to court for more rights with him. TJ, I am exhausted. I work all the time because my job is never done. I am being pulled in so many different ways that I honestly feel that there is never enough of me to go around. If I even pretend to factor in you and all that you have going on along with the safety and security of myself and my son, it becomes overwhelming, TJ. I can admit that as a woman, I cannot handle your situation. It is too much. I am not equipped." She nudged me backward and stepped out of my embrace. She turned her back to me again, looking out of the window.

I hated rejection. My knees threatened to buckle. "My whole life, I ain't never had a chance. My household was crazy. My mother was beaten every day and raped three to four times a week. My sister was raped by my father and my brothers. She was beaten into the ground by my father as well. Then when he was done beating her, he would beat me senseless.

I buried both my mother and my sister at a young age and was forced to learn how to survive in the deadliest city in America before I was even fifteen-years-old. I taught myself everything, including how to conquer a jungle of killas.

Now, everybody holds this shit against me. I didn't have a chance. My life was over the minute my mother gave birth to me." I fell to my knees, shaking. "I'm to the point where I need a reason to keep going. I wanna see that reason in my son, but as much as it pains me to admit this, I don't. I need more than that. I need more than him." I balled my fists and slammed the right one on to the carpet.

"I wish I was strong enough to pull you out of that dark abyss, TJ, but I ain't. I got the weight of the world on my shoulders. I am close to cracking. There is no way I can offer you a piece of me when I don't even know who I am. All I see right now is an unhappy mother faking the funk."

I stood up. "I will give you the world, Jelissa. Just love me. Please?"

"I'm not strong enough, TJ. Don't you get it? I am broken! How can I love and save you when I am drowning just as much as you are? Please understand me." She turned around with her eyes bucked wide open.

I was lost. I was searching for a feeling that was foreign to me. After all of the chaos and mayhem, I needed an escape. I needed a different feeling. A different path. I was crying on the inside. My heart was turning blacker and blacker by the second. I nodded my head. "Awright then, Jelissa, I understand. Just thought it would be in my best interest to ask for help when I needed it." I tried my best to gather myself.

"I'm sorry I couldn't help you. Can you close the door on your way out?" She didn't even bother to look back at me as she said these words.

"Yeah, I can do that." My eyes became glossy. "It's funny because I know that when it all boils down that you are the only woman that can help me see my purpose for being here. I'm so lost and so fucked up that all I wanna do is kill. Man, I need you, but I see what it is. Hold yo' head up, Queen. If you ever need anything, my number is the same."

I stepped out onto the porch and closed the door behind me, feeling ten times worse than when I first got to her house. I felt like I needed to release my internal pains or they were going to cause me to implode.

T.J. Edwards

Chapter 4

Two weeks after my big fail with Jelissa, Juelz pulled up in front of one the many buildings that I was trapping out of on the north side of Chicago. It was hot and humid outside. There was no wind and I was sweating worse than I could ever remember.

I had Lacey and Tonya standing on each side of me with the little mist fans that blew cool air and squirted water at the same time. Juelz pulled up in front of me after being allowed into the parking lot by my shooters, driving a cherry red Lamborghini sitting on twenty-eight inch Sprewells. The license plates read his name, and he had a bad-ass Puerto Rican broad in the passenger's seat with a plate of cocaine on her lap. She tooted up a strong line and held her right nostril, then she did the same with her left. She pinched her nose and tilted her head backward against the seats, which had Juelz's name stitched on them.

"Nigga, check me out. You see how a ma'fucka looking?" He asked, lowering his Chanel glasses. He smiled, and I saw that his entire grill was gold with diamonds all over them.

I was leaning up against my black Navigator. It was plain, but clean. The inside was decked out with white leather seats and television screens all over it. "Look like to me your silly ass setting yourself up for an indictment."

He laughed. "How the Feds gon' indict a nigga they work for?" He pulled his nose and nodded his head at the Spanish beauty sitting inside of his passenger's seat. "You like shorty?"

I eased off the front of my truck. Tonya sucked her teeth loudly and mugged the female inside of Juelz's whip. "Juelz, you always gotta bring them Spanish hoes over here to compete wit' somebody. Why don't you leave dem bitches on the north side where they belong?"

"Bitch, stay in yo' lane!" Juelz snapped at her. "What you think, dawg?"

Tonya rolled her eyes and crossed her arms. "Whatever."

I leaned into the car and looked his woman over. She was gorgeous; there was no denying that. "Where did you meet her at?"

"Humboldt Park. I just opened three traps out that way and the niggas that used to run her hood… Well, let's just say that today is their funerals. You're more than welcome to attend them if you want to," he joked. His female counterpart laughed along with him.

"Real funny, nigga. What brings you over here right now?"

I looked and saw that my killas had all three of the cars that Juelz's killas were rolling behind him, surrounded. You see, they had been given the green light to allow Juelz to enter our jungle when he came through. He was the only person outside of my crew that was able to get close to me. But his security was stopped at the entrance of the parking lot and held at gunpoint. They were granted the right to see Juelz, but that was it.

It was essential that my soldiers kept the ups on his. It wasn't that I didn't trust Juelz. He was my brother. But this was Chicago, and in this city, everybody was looking to get ahead by getting a title. My murder would ring bells out the city. Any nigga that killed me was destined to be hailed as a king of the trap. That was, until he was gunned down along with his entire family and clan. Retaliation was a guarantee.

"Yo, TJ, how did that bitch get past security anyway?" Lacey asked, shielding her eyes from the sun.

"Yeah, Juelz got the golden ticket. Not this pretty bitch," Tonya added upping her gun.

"That's a good question." I took a step back.

Lacey hurried around to Juelz's passenger's door and smacked the side of it. "Get out, bitch, you gotta be searched."

The Spanish chick looked over to Juelz for assistance. "Papi, what are they talking about?"

Juelz popped the locks and the Lamborghini door slowly ascended toward the sky. "Yo, it ain't no way around dis shit, shorty, just do what they say."

Tonya was real rough when she pulled the Latina out of the passenger's seat and flung her to the ground. "Bitch, don't move."

"What is this?" the Latina questioned.

"See, that's what you call moving. That shit'll get you killed." Tonya slammed her knee into the girl's lower back and pressed her gun to the back of her head.

Lacey spit into her hair. "Bitch ain't all that, daddy. All she got is this hair." She pulled out a switchblade, ready to cut some of it off.

Juelz looked up at me with his eyes glossy. "Nigga, you really finna let this shit happen?"

I ignored him. "Tell that bitch what she did wrong, young Queen."

Tonya rolled the female on to her side and stuffed the barrel of her gun into her mouth. She cocked the hammer. Keep in mind that it was broad daylight and all eyes were already on us because of Juelz's foreign whip that was shining like new diamonds. "Bitch, don't you ever attempt to get this close to my daddy again. This time you get a warning; next time you get smoked. You understand me good?" She pushed her gun further down the woman's throat until it affected her gag reflexes.

The Latina nodded her head with tears coming out of her eyes. "Okay!" she screamed over the barrel, her spit dripping off of it.

Lacey pulled her by her hair. She hollered out in pain. "When I let you up, you better take off running to your people over there. You got me?"

"Yeah!" she grumbled with the barrel still in her mouth.

Tonya eased her barrel out of her mouth. "Get, bitch! Go run to yo' peoples! Now!"

The Latina eased up with her face wet with tears. She looked over to Juelz for a brief second. Juelz was sipping from his bottle of Moët and acting like he was oblivious to what was going on. She stood up and took off running toward his security. When she made it to them, they allowed her to get in the car.

"I hope you bitches know that if ever y'all come out East or West to either one of my decks, you hoes gon' experience the same treatment," she promised them.

Tonya and Lacey came and stood behind me. I felt the fans on each side of me before the mist was squirted to give me further relief. The people that were watching the whole event went back about their day. The amusement was over. There was guaranteed to be more action in the night. After all, this was Chicago, and we were in the heart of the slums.

I laughed at the stupid look on Juelz's face. "You should have already known that shit was gon' take place. My Queens don't play, especially when you try and front on them with them Spanish broads. I already told you what it is wit' me."

"They just hating. Them black hoes can never hold a candle to them exotic bitches and you know it. Don't flex like Juanita wasn't killing shit."

Lacey stepped forward and cocked her .9 "Word to God, I'd splash that bitch right now if TJ gives me the word. We don't play that shit around here. That was a breach of security."

Juelz waved her off. "Shut the fuck up." He mugged her. "Yo' jealous ass. Say, TJ, I got the low down on that nigga Deion. I need for you to roll wit' me for a minute."

Just hearing Deion's name made a chill go down my spine. My sister Marie and my mother flashed into my mind. I started seeing all kinds of sick images. "When you get this information?"

"Nigga, don't worry about it. Roll wit' me for a minute so we can holler. Come on. I'll have you back before those li'l hoes get to feeling lost and shit." He mugged both Tonya and Lacey.

"Nigga, watch how yo' monkey ass handling my li'l women. They belong to me." I ain't like how my homie was trying to get down on my Queens. I felt like he was jaded because of how they treated his li'l Spanish chick.

"Bruh, you already know them li'l hoes is old news, and dis is how we talk to and about project bitches. I ain't changing for no ma'fucka. It's as simple as that."

"TJ don't run his ship like you used to, Juelz. He respects us, and because of that, it ain't a ma'fucka rolling around our hood that won't die for him. All he's doing is asking you to respect us. What's so hard about that? What, we too black or somethin'?" Lacey asked with her face balled up.

"Yo, you bitches ain't doing shit but getting beside yourselves. Don't think I won't get out of this ma'fuckin' Lam and smack both of y'all asses up. Word to the gang, ain't shit changed about me. Now keep playin'.'"

Tonya stepped closer to his whip. "You'd have to kill me. Its gang gang all ma'fuckin' day long over here. Ain't no pussy nowhere but between my legs. Fuck you think this is?"

"Right?" Lacey stepped beside her.

"What?" Juelz threw up his door and jumped out of the car. A Draco fell off of his lap and to the ground. He reached and picked it up. Once he had it in his hands, he mugged both girls and headed toward them.

I slid in front of him. "I love you, dawg, but these my li'l women. We are all family over here. Ain't no ma'fucka finna put they hands on them. Not now, not period. Let's just roll before shit gets twisted."

Juelz stepped into my face. "Blood, you finna flex on me for some hoes? Really? What type of shit is that?"

"Like I said, I love you, Juelz, but they are my family. I got them. Don't knock they heart. They ain't doing shit but marveling behind their daddy. Right girls?"

"You muthafuckin' right," they uttered in unison.

Juelz glared at them again and then back up to me. He snickered. "Yeah, awright den, TJ, let's just roll before shit gets out of hand. We don't need that happening."

I turned around and kissed both girls on the lips before sliding into Juelz's Lamborghini. "Yo, tell bruh n'em I'm rolling wit' Juelz on bidness and I'll be back in a few hours. Hit me on my Galaxy if I'm needed. Y'all watch my operations covertly and send me updates. Dismissed." I watched them nod and walk away.

Juelz pulled out of the big project parking lot. As soon as his tires hit the road to exit the hood, my shooters took their weapons off of his animals and allowed for them to pull off behind him.

Juelz was quiet for five full minutes before he turned to me and shook his head. "Shorty, you got them bitches way too comfortable. They talking shit to me and everything. Fuck that start?"

I licked up and down a Garcia Vega. That bitch was stuffed with some orange OG Kush and I was ready to put some pressure on my lungs. "Nigga, like I said before, my people act how they act because they run under me. A kingdom will always reflect its King."

"I gave you them hoes when they were just sixteen. They weren't on shit. Now they act like they are straight killas. They probably ain't even got no bodies under their belts yet, do they?"

I nodded. "A few apiece. They got more heart than some of my niggas in the family. But that's neither here nor there. What's good with Deion? What kind of drop do you got on him?"

"Yo, if you was really my nigga, you would let me kill both of them bitches for coming at me like that. I feel like a straight goofy, TJ. Let me whack them broads. Word to God, I'll replace them with two Spanish hoes that'll suck and fuck you good, and they'll bust their guns at all costs. What do you say?"

"You bugging. Let that shit ride, nigga. There ain't no harm nor disrespect. You came at them real foul and they stood on their square. It's as simple as that. Let's move on." I was starting to get irritated. I already wasn't into a nigga killing a female for no reason. I most definitely wasn't about to give my right hand man the go ahead to off a Queen from my circle. He had to be out of his mind. "Deion, nigga. Talk."

Juelz pulled his nose and sniffed real hard. "Yeah, a'ight. Look, Deion just moved up in ranks with the Dark Knight Cartel. They now use him as one of their main sources to distribute and control the dumping post in Iowa. He is one of the heads that is in charge of flooding Chicago and Gary, Indiana. I guess some major shit went down with the Feds and your brother stood his ground and didn't talk. That got Jefe Javier's attention. As you know, he is the leader of the Dark Knight's Cartel out of Mexico City, Mexico. He is the head

Chilango. Now that your brother has Javier's approval, it is going to be a little more difficult to make him pay for his sins."

"What, man? Fuck Javier and his cartel, and don't call that rapist fuck nigga my brother. You're my brother. The niggas that eat out of the dumpsters of the slums with me are my brothers. Fuck Deion. Where is he at right now?" I took the .44 Desert Eagle off of my hip and cocked it.

"Damn, bruh, calm yo' loony ass down. That nigga is visiting Mexico right now according to my sources, Javier Guzman wanted to meet him in person. He left yesterday and he ain't supposed to be back for a few weeks. They say he's getting the royal treatment down there. Treatment for a king."

I wanted to punch a hole through Juelz's windshield. "That nigga is a bitch. He ain't no king. Anybody that would do their own sister like that deserves everything that I am going to be giving to his punk ass when I catch him. Do we know where he lays his head at yet? Huh?"

"That nigga cold wit' them hide outs so you already know that's gon' take some more digging. However, Deion always had a thing for messing wit' dem li'l young broads. I'ma put the feelers out to see what I can dig up and you do the same. Don't worry, bruh, we gon' find a way to cut into that low life-ass nigga real soon. He ain't always gon' be able to hide behind the Dark Knights like he is right now."

I sat there fuming. I didn't have a full understanding as to how strong the Dark Knights Cartel was, and I didn't care either. I wanted Deion's ass. I didn't feel like Marie could rest peacefully until she knew that Deion was frying in hell alongside Kalvin.

"Yo, I'ma do some digging, too. I don't feel like my world is going to be right until that chump ain't got no more breath inside of him."

Juelz looked over at me. "Bruh, long as you know that we are in this shit together, you should be able to be easy. When we catch him, it's curtains."

T.J. Edwards

Chapter 5

Punkin called me over a week later. She opened the front door with a smile on her face when I got there. She had on a black, red, and blue sundress that was loose on her figure. Her hair was pulled back into a ponytail, and her makeup was done to accentuate the slants in her eyes. It was a warm, windy day. The sun was shining bright in the sky, and the birds were chirping loudly in a tree right next to Punkin's porch. She stepped out of the door just a little bit and pulled me inside of her hallway. Before I could fully react, she kissed my lips.

"Mmm, baby, I missed you." She rested her hands on my chest.

I grabbed her arms and moved her backward into the house. I kicked the door closed with my right blue and gray Airmax and scanned the living room. "Shorty, the last time you and I were together you were acting funny as hell. What gives now?"

She yanked her arms away from me. "Damn, TJ, why I just can't be in a good mood and thirsty to see yo' ass? Why do you always try and make it seem like I'm up to something?" She furrowed her thick eyebrows and crossed her arms in front of her chest.

"I ain't always doing nothing, but I read people real well. You ain't never called me over here on some lovey dovey shit before. Every time I came through, I always had to work for it. So what's so different right now?"

She waved me off. "You know what? Forget it. Damn. Every time we come into contact, it always gotta be some kind of drama. I was sitting here missing you and wishing I could be with you, so I called you. I was surprised when you said that you were coming right away, and even more shocked when I looked out the window and I saw your Bentley truck parking in front of the house. Look at this." She pulled up her sundress to show me her freshly shaved pussy. She ran her finger through her lips and held them out to me.

I raised my right eyebrow. "You been fuckin' wit' any nigga outside of me since Junior came into the world?"

"Really? Are we asking each other these questions right now? You know damn well you shouldn't ask me any questions you really don't want to know the answer to. Or any questions that you know you can't pass yourself."

I walked up on her and grabbed her wrist. "You heard what the fuck I asked you. Stop playin' wit' me. Answer the ma'fuckin' question." I backed her up into the wall. She crashed into it with her head against it.

No, damn. I ain't had time to focus on no man. Now can you please let my wrist go? You're hurting me."

I sucked her finger into my mouth and licked all around it to taste her. "You betta be telling the truth." My lips wound up on her neck. I kissed her there first, and then sucked hard right on the thick vein that ran the length of it.

"Mmm, I am. Ain't nobody gotta lie to you." She closed her eyes.

My right hand went under her dress and rubbed the hot, soft lips of her pussy. Two of my fingers split her crease. She was already wet. "Yo, what's good wit' you, shorty?" I slipped them into her hole and slowly began to work them in and out of her at an even pace.

"Unnn." Her fingers dug into my shoulders. "What are you talking about?" She spaced her bare feet.

I sped up the pace. "One minute you're hot, and the next you're cold wit' me. When you gon' make up your mind?" I pulled my fingers out and sucked them into my mouth.

She walked into my face and placed her forehead to my chin. "I want us to work for Junior, TJ. He deserves to have both of his parents. That's the only way that he is going to be able to make it in this cold, cold world." She unbuttoned my Polo shirt and dropped to her knees. Next came my Ferragamo belt. My Polo jeans were unfastened, then my dick was in her right hand with her pumping it like crazy. "I'm so horny for you right now. I don't know what's wrong with me." She rubbed my piece over her cheeks and kissed the head sloppily.

I braced myself with the use of the arm of the couch. Punkin went to work sucking me like a champion. I whimpered and closed my eyes tight. Every time I opened them, the sight of her doing her thing made me want to cum prematurely. I had to think about all kinds of murders and other shit - that was, until she got to lightly nipping her teeth over the head. Then I began to tremble. I backed up, and my dick popped out of her mouth loudly. "Wait a minute, baby."

She stood up sucking on her bottom lip. "You remember how we were talking about what we used to do in private when we were little?"

I nodded with my dick jumping up and down. "Yeah, what about it?"

"Well…" She pulled down the shoulder straps of her dress and allowed for them to drop to her feet. She stepped out of it and stood before me naked. Her C-cup breasts bounced. Her nipples were spiked. There were light stretch marks over them, and some across her stomach. Her hips appear wider. "When we were little and I used to watch y'all boys play basketball in the park with your shirts off, that used to drive me crazy. I'd be squeezing my thighs together, and if nobody was watching my hand would slip between my thighs just enough to touch my pearl. It used to drive me crazy though. Then when I got back home for the night I used to wear myself out thinking about what I saw."

I dropped down, rubbed her cat. I was hard as hell imagining her li'l young ass on some freaky shit because back when we were in school, Punkin used to act so innocent. I never for one second thought that she was as naughty as she was admitting to being. I licked all over her kitty, and opened the lips, revealing her glossy pink. I swiped my tongue up and down it, and dove as deep into her as my tongue could reach.

She shivered. "I was fast back then. Not with no boys or nothing like that, but I did have a few friends that I played around with. I think girls are freakier than dudes when it all comes down to it. Unnh, that feels so good."

I had her sex lips wide open, licking each side. My tongue would run circles around her clitoris and then I was sucking it like a nipple. She grabbed both sides of my face and held it while she humped into it. She was so wet that it was running down my neck.

"Unnn! Unnnn! I'm finna cum, TJ. Shit, you finna make me cum, baby." She grabbed a handful of my dreads and mashed my face into her center until she came hard, screaming at the top of her lungs. Her knees buckled. She wound up on her back with me still eating her like a hungry savage. "Wait! Wait! Uhhhhh, shit."

I held her sex lips opened wide and attacked her clitoris like it owed me money. Two fingers went into her hole at full speed, and I sucked as hard as I could. She arched her back and screamed louder than before, and then she was cumming and shaking on the carpet. I slurped and got between her thighs, sliding deep into her.

"Fuck! Here you go! Here you fuckin' go!" She stretched her arms straight out and surrendered to me.

I cocked back and slammed home as hard as I could. I repeated the same process until I was stroking her back to back while I sucked on her neck. She moaned into my ear and dug her nails into my sides. My hips kept popping forward. Our middles clapped into one another's over and over. I growled.

"TJ! TJ! Please, shit! You're killing me! Unnn! Unnn! Shit!" She wrapped her thighs around my waist and pushed at my chest as if she was trying to get me off of her.

That made me fuck her harder and faster. My back rolled, sweat appeared on the sides of my forehead. I could feel myself hitting her bottom. She sat up and smacked my face. "You're killing this pussy! Stop! Aw, fuck me!" She laid back down and closed her eyes. She squeezed her titties and pulled the erect nipples. Milk seeped out of them.

I leaned down and licked all of the liquid up, sucking one breast at a time. Milk entered into my mouth and drove me nuts. She screamed that she was cumming. I stroked faster and harder. The taste of the milk on my tongue sent me over the edge. I groaned and came, shooting deep into her wound. She dug her nails into my shoulder blades.

"Huh! Huh! Huh!" I shivered, cumming and jerking.

Punkin came and fell backward. Her face was sweaty. Her eyes were slitted. She looked up at me and wagged her index finger from side to side. "You ain't right. Damn, you ain't no good." Milk continued to seep out of her nipples onto her stomach. That shit looked so hot to me that I had to clean it up.

Later that night, we wound up crawling into her bed with me lying on my back and her lying on my chest. She rubbed up and down my stomach. "TJ, when will you be ready to come home and settle down with me? I feel like we ain't getting no younger, and more sooner than later, we are going to have to grow the hell up. I know that I can be that mother and wife that you need me to be. All I ask is that you give me a chance. I don't want no other nigga thinking he can raise our son as his own. You're his father, not nobody else."

I looked down at her. "Fuck is you saying? You saying that if I ain't ready to come home right now and settle down with just you that you gon' have some other nigga play daddy to my baby? Word to God, I'd smoke that punk and everybody else wit' his last name. Don't fuckin' play wit' me."

She hugged me closer. "Baby, I'm not saying that. What I'm saying is that I need for us to work out because I don't want our child raised in a household where either he is seeing me with another man that isn't his father, or he is seeing you with a woman that isn't me. We need to raise our baby together. It's as simple as that."

"Yo, I can be with you, Punkin, for the sake of our child, but then there is this question about the streets. You're always trying to make me leave my post in the slums when it is all that I know. I'm eating in those trenches, and I been getting it out the mud since I was a young nigga. Do you think you can accept that?"

She sighed. "I don't know. I might have to. It seems like there is always somethin' or someone in the way that will prevent me from having all of you, and I can't make them all disappear. Lord knows I've been trying." She was quiet. "Anyway, do you see yourself ever leaving the streets though? Like maybe even a year from now?"

"I don't know. Only God knows the answer to that question. I guess we'll see."

"Then I guess I'ma have to give you the benefit of the doubt that you know what you are doing in them. I don't want you to be out there, and I honestly don't know if I could do the whole jail thing, but if it comes with the territory, I might have to try." She kissed my chest. "I hope I ain't just feeling this way because you dug me out either." She snickered.

"Yeah, I hope not either." I was quiet for a moment. I didn't know if I wanted to be some house nigga that was locked down and up under the same female all day every day. That shit seemed boring to me, especially since me and Punkin were always arguing.

My phone rang, and before I could get to it, Punkin grabbed it off of the night stand and looked at the face. "Jelissa? Who is this bitch?"

I grabbed the phone out of her hand and placed the phone to my ear. "What's good, shorty?"

"I need you to come over here right now, please. I'm messed up, and I just need some company," Jelissa whimpered into the phone.

I hopped out of the bed and started to get dressed. "I'll be there in twenty minutes. Okay?"

"Yes. I'll be here, and thank you." She hung up.

"Where the fuck you think you finna go?" Punkin got out of the bed naked.

I kept getting dressed. "I gotta handle some bidness. I'll fuck wit' you later."

"So you finna just up and leave?" She grabbed my arm.

I pulled away from her. "Calm yo' li'l ass down. I'll be back, damn."

"TJ, if you leave, you better stay yo' ass over there wit' that bitch. Don't come back here. I mean that."

I tucked my pistol on my hip. "Shut the fuck up. I said I'll be back. Quit being so ma'fuckin' extra."

"Fuck you! Don't bring your ass back to my house tonight. I promise you won't be getting in. Junior is with my mother until Monday anyway, so guess there ain't no reason for you to be here."

I opened the front door after gathering all my stuff. "Yo, I love you, Punkin. We honestly need to talk about how we are going to coexist together. I hate arguing wit' you all the time. That's getting old."

"Nawl, what's getting old is you always running away before we can get a clear understanding about things. Real men don't run away from their problems, especially when their problems circle around their child and the mother of their child. You ain't nothing but a grown-ass boy. Ugh! I hate that I had a baby by yo' ass!"

I rushed into the house, ready to snatch her ass up. She swung and busted me right in the lip. Then she backed up and threw up her guards.

"What you wanna do? Huh? I ain't scared of you. You wanna kill me like you do everybody else, then do it. I ain't afraid!" She stood naked, seemingly ready to go.

I touched my lip and saw the blood on my fingers. My vision started to go cloudy. Suddenly, I felt like murdering Punkin. I didn't allow for nobody to cause me to bleed without me sending them to the Reaper. My body grew goosebumps all over it. I eyed her and immediately saw her laying in a coffin. Had it not been for the milk that began to seep out of her nipples, once again reminding me that she had given my son life, I was sure that I would have slumped her while I was in my state of psychosis. Instead, I nodded my head and closed her front door behind me.

"I hate you, Jahrome!" she snapped, calling me by my middle name.

A loud bang came from the door, but I didn't care, I was rushing to my Bentley truck. I needed to get to Jelissa as soon as possible.

Chapter 6

When Jelissa opened the door to her duplex, I wanted to run around Chicago and start shooting ma'fuckas down just so I could release the anger surging inside of me just from the mere sight of her.

She had a blackened left eye. Her top lip was slightly swollen, and there were scratches across her neck along with fingerprints. My heart sank. I picked her up and carried her inside of the house, feeling sick to my stomach.

"Jelissa, what happened?" My blood began to boil. She looked so delicate and helpless.

"I didn't wanna call you, TJ, but all of my family is in New Jersey. I needed somebody. He messed me up for no reason." She broke down crying and hugged my neck.

Damn, I felt like shit. I held her tighter and allowed for her to cry into the crux of my neck for as long as she needed to. I rubbed her back and bounced her slightly up and down as if she was a little baby or something. I just wanted her to calm down and to know that I was there and I had her back. "Who did this to you?"

"Deion. He was here an hour or so ago. He took Rae'Jon and said that he dared me to call the police. He said that if I did, he would kill me. I believe him." She cried harder.

My face dropped. I carried her to the couch and sat down on it. I kissed the side of her neck. "Baby, please stop crying. You making me wanna kill a ma'fucka. Now stop, I'm begging you. Why would Deion do this?"

She was quiet with the exception of her whimpering. "I don't know. He was all high off of that dope. He sat right there on my couch and shot up. I think he is out of his mind." She snuggled her face into my collarbone. "Can you chill here with me for a few hours just in case he comes back? Plus, I need you to stop me from calling the police. I don't know what he is going to do with my son, but I can't help but to think the worst." She hugged me tighter. "What should I do?"

I was so mad that I wanted to holler at the top of my lungs. Deion's bitch ass was always attacking women. I hadn't ever heard about him slumping no real killas in the streets. He was a pussy, if you asked me, just like Kalvin. Both of those niggas were foul. "Do you know where he lays his head? Have you ever been to his house?"

She shook her head. "I didn't even know that he knew where I lived. When he showed up on my doorstep, I felt like I had seen a ghost. He beat on the door harder until I opened it. As soon as I did, he came in and started beating me up. Rae'Jon tried to help me, and he knocked my baby out." She cried harder. "He-he-he let him sleep right there on the floor until he shot up his dope, beat me some more, and then left with Rae'Jon draped over his shoulder like a hunting game. I don't know what to do." She hugged my body and cried on my chest until my shirt was soaked. I held her for a full hour, just letting her cry. I didn't have the words to say to her. Deion was my brother, but we weren't family. I wanted to smoke his ass after I tortured him for his sins. He'd hurt so many innocent women that it was sickening.

After Jelissa cried herself out for a straight ninety minutes, she calmed down, and climbed off of my lap. She stood in front of me and wiped her tears away. "TJ, there is something that I gotta tell you that I should have told you from the jump, but I didn't want to ruin our chances at friendship or anything like that. There are two reasons why I've been hesitant to start anything with you, and why I've been so up and down when it comes to you."

I stood up and looked down on her. I held her face with my hands. Jelissa was so flawlessly fine to me. So small, so delicate, so demure. Her proper talking was also alluring and appealing to that street savage inside of me. "Talk to me."

She held my waist. "Well, one of the reasons I've been so fearful of starting anything with you is because of your bloodline. I've been in a short relationship with your brother and it was terrible for me. His temper is quick and explosive. He is too hard to ever be soft with me, and he is abusive. So was your father, as far as I have gathered, so I could only imagine that over time, you would become the same way. I like you, but I have to admit that these factors scare the heck out of me."

I kissed her puffy top lip softly. "That's understandable, but I am nothing like them. Kalvin isn't my biological father, and Deion was born from Satan. I ain't got shit in common wit' either one of them niggas. But go on. What's the second reason?" I kissed her forehead. I was six-foot-two and Jelissa was five-foot-four. I towered over her and she always seemed so precious to me, despite our circumstances.

She took another deep breath and lowered her head. "Damn, please don't be mad at me for keeping this from you, because it is a game changer."

I picked her chin up and kissed her lips. "It's okay. Talk to me. Please, baby." Another kiss landed on her cheek.

"Okay, well, damn." She was quiet again. She eased out of my embrace and sat across the room from me. Tears ran down her cheeks. She covered her face with her hands. "TJ, me and Deion have a one-year-old son together. His name is A'Jhani, and I had him in Newark. I never brought him back to Chicago because ever since he has been born, I have been struggling with whether I want to keep him or not. Your brother forced himself on me and impregnated me. Every time I see our son, all I can do is think about how he came to be, and what man I had him with. It is painful and I feel so horrible. Deion found out about him and now he is demanding that I give him his son. He said that I would never see Rae'Jon again until I traded him for A'Jhani. I don't know what to do right now."

I sat there stuck. I frowned and tried to think back when I had first met Jelissa. It was definitely a little more than a year ago, and now that I thought about it, she was pregnant. Damn, how did I miss that? I shook myself out of my zone when she fell to the floor and placed her forehead on the carpet. I got up and came beside her.

"Jelissa, come here. Get up." I pulled her to her feet. I guided her arms to wrap around me. I kissed her cheek. "I got you, li'l baby. I'm here for you and I ain't going nowhere. I'ma help you get Rae'Jon back, and I'ma get rid of that nigga for good. You got my word on that. Don't you worry about a ma'fuckin' thing. You hear me?"

She nodded. "Yes, and thank you, TJ. I don't know why you care about me so much, but thank you."

I picked her up and carried her to the back bedroom. I laid her on the bed, and kissed her lips. "I'll be right back." I checked and locked every window in the house and both doors. Then I sent word to my security team that was stationed outside of her place to be on high alert and to wet anything that looked suspicious. After all of that was taken care of, I hopped into Jelissa's shower for ten minutes. When I came back into her room, she was curled into a ball sucking her thumb.

"My whole life I have always struggled with severe depression. That's why it's so hard for me to put on and keep on weight. I don't know what Deion is doing to my son, but I swear I won't be able to think clearly until Rae'Jon is back safe and sound in my arms."

I slipped behind her and pulled her back to my chest. She was so little compared to my muscular frame. "I got you. String that nigga along for a week at the most and I promise you that we are going to have your son back around that time. I need for you to keep hope and faith in me. Can you do that?"

"I only trust in the Lord. The Bible says that men will fail you. I love Jesus, and I know that He will never leave or forsake me. I have to believe like I've never believed before that Jehovah will deliver myself and my son from the Lion's Den. Can you hold me tighter?"

I scooted forward until her backside was in my lap. All I had on was a pair of boxers. I held her protectively. "It's cool then, you can believe in your Bible and I am going to believe in the power of this gun. That nigga ain't gon' do all of the shit that he did and get away with it. You know how God be getting niggas back and all of that for the wrongs that they have done?"

"Yeah, the Word says that if you live by the sword, you will die by the sword. It also says that you will reap whatever you sow."

"What does that mean?" I was confused. It sounded kind of weird to me.

"It's saying that whatever you put out into the world, it will always come back to you. So if you plant seeds of evil and death, eventually those seeds will blossom and overcome you. I have no doubt that God has a divine plan for Deion. He is too wicked and sick. All I hope is that he doesn't meet his demise before I get my son back. That would shatter me."

"What are you going to do about the other one?"

"The other what?"

"Son. Didn't you say that you and him have a son and he is in Newark with your mother?"

"Aw, yeah, what do you mean what am I going to do about him?"

"You don't want him. Sooner or later that child is going to need your love and compassion. He can't be held responsible for how he was brought into this world. You can't hate him because of his ratchet-ass father. He needs you."

"Yeah, I know. I'll get there." She exhaled loudly. "Do you still care about me?"

"Yeah." I kissed the back of her neck.

"How do you feel about being with me now though? Is that even still an option?"

"Yeah, I like you, and you make me feel some type of way. I don't care about your past. I can't hold that against it? Besides, A'Jhani gon' need a man in his life that understands his bloodline. That's me. I gotta help him to break that cycle, just like I have to with my own son."

"What about your own son? Are you and Punkin going to be together? Be honest."

"I don't know. Right now we ain't, and if things get serious with you, we most definitely won't."

She fidgeted. "Is that fair though?"

"Is what fair?"

"You being with me instead of her. Doesn't she need you? I know firsthand how hard it is to raise a son on your own without the father. Have you considered getting things right with her?"

"Shit, just crash right now. Besides, I'm here with you, Jelissa, can't we just be?"

She sat all the way up and looked at me with a serious expression on her face. She slid out of the bed and clicked on the lamp. Her fingers roamed through her hair. She appeared lost and hurt. Her injuries were more visible now that the light was on.

I could already tell that something wasn't right, so I sat up. "What's up, shorty?"

"I don't know what Punkin is telling you, but I promise you that she is going through it right now. Damn." She punched her fist.

"What's the matter?"

"You are, and all men like you." She pointed at me and blinked tears down her cheeks. "Y'all don't understand how hard it is out here for us single mothers, especially the black ones.

We are forced to raise little black boys on our own, boys that will be targeted by the world as soon as they begin to hit puberty. There is only so much a mother can teach her son. It is important for you men to be exactly what you are supposed to be, which is grown-ass men. Got this idiot coming over here and beating me in the ground with no regard to the fact that I gave life to his child.

That doesn't even matter. It doesn't matter to him. It doesn't matter to Rae'Jon's father, and clearly it doesn't matter to you, because if it did, you wouldn't be here right now. You would be laid up with your son's mother trying to figure out how y'all could come together as parents to make sure that your son has as many opportunities in this world as possible. Damn, you shouldn't be here right now." She walked to the bedroom door and opened it.

"Jelissa, calm the fuck down, shorty. You are going from zero to a hunnit for no reason. I didn't come here so I could crap on Punkin. I am here because you say that you needed company, so I busted my ass to get here. Now that I am here, that shit ain't fair for you to try and kick a nigga to the curb like you always do. Let's get an understanding for and of each other. Is that so hard?"

She closed her eyes and lowered her head. "Was you with her before you came here? And please don't lie to me, TJ. Matter of fact, I'ma make this very easy. Did you sleep with another woman before you got over here to me?" She opened her eyes and looked over at me.

My brain felt like it was getting close to shutting down. It got so scrambled that I simply copped out and grew angry. "Why does that even matter?"

"Answer the question, TJ."

"Nawl. What type of sense would that make?" I lied, standing up and walking over to her.

She held up her hand. "I'ma ask you one more time and before you respond, I need you to know this. Anytime a lie is exposed, it causes a real woman to question every truth. So please take your time and be honest with me. It will get you a long way. Now were you with somebody else before you got over here to me?"

Chapter 7

I was stuck. I felt like she knew something that I didn't know, so I began to nod my head slowly. "Yeah, I was."

She crossed her arms. "What made you lie to me the first time, and was that the first lie that you've ever told me?"

"I was dishonest with you because I ain't want you looking at me all funny. I didn't want you judging me. But the truth is I was with somebody else, and I rushed right over from there to you as soon as you said that you needed me. Damn, don't that count for something?"

Jelissa wiped tears from her cheeks. "Who were you with? The truth." She sniffled. Her caramel nose was slightly reddened.

"Punkin."

"Exactly. And what would make you jump out of the bed with Punkin and rush over here to me with you still smelling like sex? What, TJ?"

"Honestly?"

She gave me an exasperated sigh. "Yeah."

"You."

"Here we go with this bull crap." She walked out of the room and into the kitchen.

I followed her and pulled her arm until she was facing me. "Listen to me, Jelissa, I ain't never lied to you before. I ain't never saw the reason to. I'm sorry for doing it just then and I swear on my soul that I will never lie to you again." She tried to pull away, but I kept hold of her. "Jelissa, I came because I thought that somethin' was wrong with you. And when I first saw how messed up you were because of Deion, I ain't been able to think about nothing else but murder ever since then. I feel like that nigga put his hands on me. I will never let him or nobody else ever hurt you as long as I can prevent it. Don't you see that I care about you? Why are you making this so hard on me?"

She wiped her cheeks again. "Because right now it ain't about you, TJ. It's about Punkin, and it's about me. Us struggling, single black mothers. How in the hell can you care so much about me and I have two kids that aren't yours, yet she has one that is yours and you ain't even trying to be with her? That makes no sense."

I released her and turned my back to her. When she said those things out loud, they really made me think. Maybe she was right. It didn't make any sense. Why was I there just then? Why wasn't I at Punkin's trying to make things right?"

"You men have it way too easy. You can get a woman pregnant and then bounce once your seed has been planted with no regard for her or the child's welfare as it gets older. All most of you care about is the moment whereas us women have to live with the consequences of our actions for the rest of our lives. So does our child. Then y'all wonder why so many women are turning to each other."

"Yo, it's good, Jelissa. I fucked up. I shouldn't be here. I'ma holler at you later." She had me feeling like shit. I walked back into the bedroom and slipped on my clothes. I grabbed my pistol from under her pillow and my Bentley keys off of her dresser.

She appeared in the doorway. "So you just gon' run?"

"What?"

"You heard me. Are you just going to run out of here without explaining yourself?"

"Ain't shit to explain. I made a mistake. You're right. You have two kids by two niggas that you need to get shit right with. Punkin has one by me, and I need to get things right with her so that we can come together and give our child the best possible foundation that he can have. It takes a village, right?" I brushed past her.

She followed me down the hallway. "You still didn't explain to me why you came. How could you care so much about me when she is still in the picture?"

I headed toward the front door. "I ain't never had a red heart. My shit always been black. I don't know; there is something about you that makes me feel good inside. I feel good, and possessive at the same damn time. I think that you are the most beautiful woman I have ever laid my eyes on, and out of every woman that I have ever come across, you are my physical type.

I love your voice, your eyes, your walk, your shape, and your mind. I feel a way when you laugh, and I wanna kill a nigga when I see you cry. Even though I don't know what the fuck I'm doing or feeling right now, I can say with certainty that I love you. That is what it is, and that's why I came here tonight. Bye, Jelissa. I'ma make sure that my security stays posted all night. If that nigga come back, they gon' shoot his ass dead with no hesitation." I pulled her to me and kissed her forehead, and then I was gone.

I felt sick to my stomach. I wanted to stay with her, but she had shattered my pride by speaking her facts, comparing herself and Punkin. What kind of man was I? This is where having a real father would have helped me most significantly, but since I didn't, I was forced to question my own character and reasoning behind the things I did when it came to both Jelissa and Punkin.

***

"So you're telling me that you wanna try for real? Am I supposed to believe that? TJ, I am willing to bet my right arm that you just came from some bitch's crib. You don't even smell like the soap in my bathroom, so where did you wash up?" Punkin stood in front of me while I sat on the couch with Jelissa heavily on my mind. Damn, I wished that I would have explained myself more to her. I didn't fight hard enough, and I wanted her so bad. I still couldn't understand why.

Punkin snapped her fingers in my face. "Hello? Can you hear me talking to you?"

I moved her hands and stood up. "Look, man, I ain't been doing what I'm supposed to be doing when it comes to you. You are a Queen, Punkin. You gave me my first child. You nursed him inside of your body, and for that, I am forever in debt to you. I wanna make things right from here on out. Give me the chance to do so."

She turned her hand backwards and placed it on my forehead. "Father in heaven, is this boy sick? Did you strike him wit' lightning? What is going on with you, man?" she asked, laughing.

I moved her hand. This was becoming difficult for me. I didn't want her. I wanted the forbidden fruit that was Jelissa, but I had to see this through because Punkin had my son. Isn't that what Jelissa said? "Quit playin' wit' me. I'm trying to take all of this seriously. Now, would you please sit down with me so we can get an understanding?"

"Ain't no need to sit down. I love you, TJ, and I would very much like it if you and I left this ratchet-ass city behind so we could go somewhere nice and raise our son together. He deserves the best, and so do we. The question is if you think that both he and I are worth it enough to leave all of this behind so that we can move on to greener pastures where we are family-first focused. I am willing to do it if you are."

I was so defeated that I didn't know what to say at that moment. "I'm wit' whatever. Just give me a second to think about everything."

"What do you need a second for? You just made it seem like you had everything figured out. Now, when I come around and am ready to take that step, you need a second to think. What the fuck are you doing?"

"Yo, Punkin, chill, man. Got damn. I just need to hear myself think for a second."

"Why do you have an attitude? What is going on with you?"

I closed my eyes and tried to make sense of things. I was wondering, if I had a legit father, what would he have told me to do in that moment, or my mother? Would she have told me to go over and fight for Jelissa because that is who I truly wanted to be with? Wouldn't she have asked me why I wanted to be with her, and if it would have been a good idea?

After all, she did have a son with Deion. Wasn't that something like incest if I was to turn around and be with her? I mean, we had already been sexually intimate. I didn't know, but my feelings were so strong. I couldn't help but to crave the woman that always kept my brain working. The forbidden jewel. The small version of my mother. Damn, why did she have to be so fine and make me think so much?

"You know what, TJ? If you're going to just sit there and not answer any of my questions, then maybe we shouldn't be together, not even for Junior." She walked away from me and headed toward the back of her home.

I remained seated on the couch. My phone buzzed. I didn't even take the time to look at the face. I was too mentally gone. When Punkin came back into the room and stood in front of me, I neglected to look up at her. Instead, I pulled out a Garcia

Vega that was stuffed with some good Kush and sparked that big boy.

She remained looking down on me like I had lost my mind. "Where do you see yourself five years from now?"

I sucked in a thick cloud of Ganja. It burned my chest and caused my throat to tighten. I blew the smoke toward the ceiling. "Rich."

She rolled her eyes. "Of course you were going to say that, but I mean where, like what are you doing?"

"Rolling a Wraith with the tags out. Pink slip status. Five years from now, I'm trying to have a mansion out in Miami and workers all over the United States. I'm thinking of kingpin status. Black card eligible." I began puffing my bud again with a smile on my face as I imagined it. I knew I was destined to be a rich nigga. That broke shit didn't compliment my make-up as a man.

"You see, all of that stuff that you're speaking of isn't real. It's a fairy tale. How in the hell are you going to be driving a three hundred thousand dollar car with a mansion in Miami?"

"Because I was born to be a boss. I come from nothing. The only direction that God has ever given me is up. I was only able to be a worker for so long before I became my own boss. I conquer shit. That's what I do. I rise to power. I ain't never let anybody tell me what I couldn't achieve. I just did it, and I ain't never gave up on nothing. If I say I'ma have a mansion in Miami and a Wraith, I'ma have that shit."

Punkin smacked her lips. "Yeah, okay, so what are we doing? Are we going to be together for the long haul or what?" Right after she finished her sentence, her doorbell rang. "Who the hell is that?" She looked down at me and I jumped up, taking my pistol out of the small of my back.

The doorbell rang again.

"Yo, who the fuck ringing yo' doorbell at one in the morning?" I cut the lights and dropped low to the floor, ready to get on bidness.

"I don't know, but why are you doing all that?" She started to panic.

"Get yo' ass on the floor right now and stop making all of that ma'fuckin' noise. Come here." I grabbed her and pulled her closer to me on the floor.

"Why are we getting down like this? Why can't I just answer the door?" She jumped up and rushed to the door before I could grab her. She pulled back the curtain to the window and cursed under her breath. "I already know it's gonna be some bullshit. Fuck."

Chapter 8

Punkin's cousin Reggie stood staring at me from across the living room with a mug on his face. He was rocking a white T-shirt and I could see the handle of his gun poking up against the cloth. He sucked his gold teeth and looked me off.

"I thought you said you told yo' baby daddy that you didn't want him to come back this way tonight? How is he in this joint?" He asked these questions looking down to Punkin, who'd spent a full ten minutes begging me not to buck his ass down. She didn't open the door until I swore on our son that I wouldn't kill him.

"Say, nigga, you got any questions 'bout me, you can address me wit' them ma'fuckas. Don't be asking my BM shit. What the fuck is you doing here this late at night? It's past one, homeboy." I felt my blood pressure rising.

I didn't like Reggie's bitch ass. He was one of those cocky dudes that acted like he couldn't get whooped, although I'd already checked his history in the streets and came to find out that he was just a regular old broke-ass jack boy that travelled back and forth from Iowa to Illinois. He had a whole list of killas looking for his ass, and sooner or later, he was going to meet his Maker, especially if he kept mugging me like he was doing.

"I came over here 'cause my cousin texted me earlier saying she ain't wanna be alone. I had some shit to do at the time, but I'm here now. What's it to you?" Reggie wiped his mouth and allowed for his hand to rest by his gun.

I peeped his antics real quick. I stepped forward and nudged Punkin out of the way. "I don't know what you thought this was, homie but you gotta go. My bitch doesn't need you here to protect her. That's what she got me for."

"Psst." He snickered and crossed his arms over his chest. "You the same nigga that she trying to escape right now. If anybody about to bounce, it's you, trust and believe that." He looked over to Punkin. "Man, shorty, tell dis nigga what it really is."

Punkin looked like she was about to have a nervous breakdown. "Y'all need to chill out, damn. I don't feel like going through this shit tonight." She started to bite on her fingernails, which was odd because I could tell that they were freshly done.

"Look, I came all the way over here and I ain't trying to go nowhere for the night. Chicago PD out there lurking like crazy. I ain't trying to have them pull me over and fuck me up real bad. Plus, I'm still on federal probation." Reggie adjusted the gun on his waist and checked the time on his watch.

"All that sounds like a personal problem to me, potna. Yo, Punkin, tell yo' po'-ass cousin his goofy ass gotta go. On gang, I ain't finna keep playing these games wit' his coo ass." In Chicago, when somebody called you a coo, they were basically calling you soft, or a pussy.

"Coo? Nigga, you don't even know me like that. I get down in these streets. You ain't the only nigga wit' clout," Reggie snapped.

"What, nigga? If you don't get yo' bum ass up out of my BM shit, we gon' have some serious problems. I ain't 'bout to tell you again."

Reggie slid his hand under his shirt. "Dawg, I'm telling you, it ain't sweet. You ain't finna ho' me. She called me over here, and I'm here. However you feel under that sucka fa love umbrella is on you."

Punkin stepped in between us. "Damn, why don't y'all chill the hell out? It ain't even all that serious. Just one big misunderstanding." She spaced her arms so that we were slightly apart.

I mugged Reggie, and then a smile spread across my face. I was gon' get his ass. Even though he didn't pull the pistol out on me, he still clutched it under his shirt like he wanted to, and in Chicago, that was good enough to say that you were ready to take my life, so I had to get his ass for that. "You know what, Reggie? You are Punkin's cousin and I'm bogus for giving you a hard time. That's my fault. If she called you over here, then it ain't on you, it's on her."

He nodded his head and tried to look hard. "Dat's all I'm saying. Don't try and get up wit' me. You gotta stand on her." He looked down to Punkin.

She placed her hand on her hip and mugged him. "Nigga, oh really, dat's how you finna throw me under the bus?" She rolled her eyes. "Whatever. Look, clearly both of y'all ain't about to stay here tonight, so which one of you is about to leave?"

I raised my hand. "I'm out. Y'all family and you always supposed to ride wit' your family. It's good." I hugged Punkin briefly, grabbed all of my stuff, and bounced from her crib.

I was gon' get Reggie's ass, that was for sure, but it would happen on my own time.

***

That night, I grabbed a bottle of Hennessey and went to Forest Homes Cemetery where my mother was buried. It was a cool night, so I threw my Marc Jacobs leather on and slid down her tombstone with my back to it. I twisted the cap off of the bottle and poured a bit of it out for her memory and for all of the li'l homies that had been killed in the hood over the last few months.

I still couldn't believe that my Queen was gone. Thirty-four years old was young. It wasn't fair, especially since she had never been able to enjoy life in the least bit. I turned around and kissed her headstone, rubbing my fingers against her birthdate and death date. Tears slowly came out of my eyes and down my cheeks. I closed my lids.

"Mama, I feel so alone, and so lost right now, I don't know what to do." I drank from the bottle, guzzling until I felt like I needed to breathe.

The wind blew, and I could feel the alcohol already beginning to take over my brain. I cried harder. "This world feels like it's getting the best of me. I'm tired of all of this stuff, Ma. I ain't saying that I'm ready to die, but I'm ready for a change. I have a son now. I don't know if you knew that or not." I took another swallow from the bottle and wiped my mouth with the back of my hand. "Yeah, he's about to be one years old soon, and me and his mother barely get along. I don't know if I wanna be with her like that. I know I should be for my son, but my heart ain't really in it." I was quiet.

I looked around the graveyard. It was dark. My security walked around it with guns in their hands and red rags covering half of their faces. Both Tonya and Lacey were present. Both were double breasted. Their faces were half-covered by black masks with rhinestones all over them.

I drank from the bottle again and put the cap back on it. Then I turned around and knelt with my forehead to the dirt. "Mama, I killed Kalvin. I killed Demetrius and next, I gotta have Deion. He killed Marie, Mama, and I gotta take him out of the game for that. I don't know why our family has to go through all of this, but this is what it is. I'm all alone. My heart is cold. All I can think about all day long is murder, you, and Marie. I miss you so much." I kissed her tombstone again and broke down with my face in the dirt. I felt weak and angry at the same time. I sat on my haunches.

Juelz came out of the shadows and stood behind me. "Had to come out to see the old lady, huh?" He knelt down beside me and kissed her tombstone.

"Yeah, dawg, I'm missing my Queen. It feels like she's been gone a million years. I ain't got nobody right now, and I need my mother. She was my rock."

"You got me." Juelz placed his hand on my shoulder. "She was the only mother that I really knew. While my people were doing that dope, arguing and fighting all of the time, Deborah was making sure that I had a hot meal and clean clothes. Whenever she washed y'all shit out in her tub, she washed mine too and dried it right in front of the heater vent. Yo', I loved her more than I love my own mother."

I nodded my head. "She was thirty-four years old, shorty. Thirty-four. In all of those years, she ain't never been able to see anything of substance. My mother struggled every single day of her life. She ain't never had shit. It's no wonder why all I want to be is rich. I wanna make sure that if I die young that I have the chance to see the world some more, Juelz. Word to God, man, Chicago ain't got shit to offer a ma'fucka but heartache and pain. I was born into misery and I still ain't conquered it yet."

"Nigga, we was born into misery, and we as brothers ain't conquered it yet. I been on the front lines with you ever since we stepped out of the Cabrini Green Projects starry-eyed and ready to murder. We were shoulder to shoulder and back to back. Whenever I hear you say that you ain't got nobody or that you are alone, it kills me. You got me, shorty. I'm yo' ma'fuckin' kin." He pulled me closer to him with one arm.

I sighed and allowed for him to hug me with one arm before I started to feel weird. Juelz was my dude, but I wasn't with all of that closeness or displays of affection toward my niggas. That shit seemed too feminine to me.

I eased his arm off of my shoulder and stood up to end this whole moment we were having. "It's all good though, bruh. I know I got you and I do need to stop saying that. We've been there for each other since day one. I appreciate that sentiment." I gave him a half of a hug.

He hugged me back and took the bottle of Hennessey out of my hand, tossing it back, guzzling like he was dying of thirst. When he finished, he burped and tried to hand me back the bottle. I pushed his hand away. I didn't drink after nobody. I thought that shit was gross. I didn't like smoking behind nobody either unless it was a female I was seriously involved with.

"Yo, so what's the word? What brings you out here tonight?"

"I've been trying to locate yo' ass for the last few hours. You act like you don't know how to pick yo' phone up." He frowned and adjusted his glasses.

"What's up? Why were you looking for me?" I looked down at my mother's tombstone again and grew depressed. A hug from her would have made all of the difference.

I think I was struggling because I had so many bodies under my belt and it felt like the souls of those murdered victims were haunting me. There was also the loose end of Deion, and the fact that I needed advice because I wanted to pursue Jelissa so badly, even though she already had a son by my brother.

No matter how hard I tried to get her out of my system, I just couldn't. I felt like I was going crazy and if my mother were alive, she would have been able to give me the right advice on how to either move forward with pursuing Jelissa,

70

or how to let her go mentally. Punkin was a whole 'nother story.

"That nigga Killa Kam sent for us. He and the Coke Kings are having a major bash back out in New York, and he sent us an invitation. Everybody that's anybody is going to be there. He talked about shutting down the whole city for two nights. It's gon' be all types of foreign bitches and everything. Yo, we gotta go out there to see what it do and to show New York how we get down out here in the Windy City. You're my right hand man. We gotta put on for Chicago."

Even though partying was the last thing that I felt like doing, I needed a change of pace and scenery. "When is he supposed to be doing this?"

"It starts next Friday and goes until Monday morning. Are you wit' me or what?"

I weighed the pros and cons real fast in my head and decided a short vacation was what I needed. "Yeah, shorty, I'm there. Let's show the NY how we really get down back here in the Land." I smiled and we hugged.

Over Juelz's shoulder, I could see my mother's tombstone and it saddened me. I thought about Marie and my mood sunk even lower. I needed an escape, and New York just might be what I was missing.

T.J. Edwards

Chapter 9

When I pulled into New York City eight days later, I had Tonya riding in the front seat of the all-black-on-black Wraith that I'd rented. Juelz knew the dealer so he had the man fix up the whip to make it seem as if I'd actually bought the car. I had regular plates on it and the pink slip, though I was made to sign an agreement saying that I was only renting the car for three days. Whatever. All I know is that ma'fucka was cleaner than an old lady's kitchen. The interior was all red leather. It was spacious like a spaceship or something.

Lacey had to go to her grandfather's funeral back in Kansas and was sick as hell that she had to miss our New York outing. Tonya told her that she would go to the funeral with her, but Lacey had declined, saying that Tonya needed to watch me to make sure that none of those New York broads snatched me up or made me forget about them. I knew that would never happen. I was a diehard Chicago nigga through and through. I would never turn my back on my roots.

So I cruised through the Big Apple with my trunk knocking as if there was a whole-ass band inside of it. Tonya was fitted in Fendi, and I was dressed down in Chanel. Even my glasses were Double C. My neck was glazed in gold, and the diamonds in my earlobes cost me fifteen thousand a piece. I was fresh as newly-baked bread.

Tonya smiled over at me from her passenger's seat. "Daddy, you over there looking good as a muthafucka. You bet' not get out here and start acting all brand-new." She grabbed her small bottle of Moët from the console.

"You already know I'm finna show my ass. These Chanel jeans already fitting a li'l snug on a nigga." I laughed.

"Awright, you show yo' ass too much and one of these East Coast hoes gon' think it's sweet until I blow they shit back. I ain't scared to pull a 9-1 out here. You already know how you trained me."

In Chicago, the code word for murder was 9-1. The police used it whenever they came on a crime scene to report a homicide, so naturally we picked up their lingo in the slums.

I squeezed her thick li'l thighs. "Daddy ain't gon' make you do all of that. Just be smooth and stay in yo' lane. I'm Chiraq through and through." One of the many nicknames for Chicago was Chiraq because it was a blend of Chicago and Iraq. They called my city a warzone, just like they referred to Iraq over in the Middle East.

"Yeah, okay, long as you know. You want me to give you some head while you're rolling? I already know you tryna be on yo' boss shit."

"Shorty, you already know." I scooted back my seat and adjusted the steering wheel.

Tonya unzipped me and licked her lips. She pulled my dick out, stroking him while she looked up at me. "Let me get you right real fast." She leaned over and went to work.

I needed to see that fat ass, so as she was hunched over, I pulled her skirt up so I could see that red thong slicing her chunky ass cheeks.

She was getting thicker the older she got. She was still young, but ready. My fingers moved her thong to the side and got to playing wit' her sex lips before my fingers slipped into her to encourage her li'l young ass to suck this dick the right way. In a matter of minutes, she was moaning and slurping like her life depended on it. I sat back like a boss as I rolled through the city, appreciating the tall buildings and the array of foreign goddesses that walked the streets.

New York seemed packed and very dirty. There was litter everywhere along with crowds of people that seemed as if they were in a rush. You had dudes trying to sell you something on every corner and females selling pussy or Avon walking up and down the avenues. Most of the cars were foreign, and the majority of the people I saw were dressed in designer clothes. The city was fast, I could tell that just by rolling through it.

I wound up fingering Tonya so fast and hard, telling her that she was nasty for letting her daddy play in her pussy, that she wound up cumming and screaming before I got the chance to bust. She was licking all over my neck saying how much she loved me. I couldn't do anything but laugh, and put my dick up. She sucked my fingers clean, then wiped them and herself down with wet wipes.

We pulled up in Harlem twenty-five minutes later, right on 140th and St. Nicolas. Kammron already had the street blocked off. He was sitting on the hood of a red and pink Hellcat that was glistening in the sunlight. The outside of the Hellcat was all red, and the interior was bubblegum pink.

Behind him were all kinds of other foreign whips and trucks with niggas standing beside them with four and five gold ropes and iced-out charms and pieces. Kammron hopped off of the hood of his Hellcat fitted in a pink and red Roberto Cavalli 'fit, over pink Balenciaga's with the red bottoms. His belt was Ferragamo, and he had on so much jewelry that the old jack boy spirit in me wanted to come to the forefront. He was fresh.

I stepped out of my Wraith and gave Juelz, who was fitted in Burberry from head to toe, a half a hug. Our iced chains nearly got tangled up. "You see this nigga rocking this pink, bruh?"

"Yeah, bruh flamboyant like that. Ain't nobody fuckin' wit' Kammron when it comes to the dressing shit. At least, that's what a few hoes I fuck wit' from out dis way say. Dis nigga is a legend." Juelz nodded his head at Kammron.

Kammron placed his arm around a short, stocky nigga with caramel skin and deep waves and made his way over to us. He shook up with Juelz first, and then me. "What it do, Chiraq? Y'all most definitely in the building, word up." He checked out our fly and stood back. "Two thumbs up. Both of you niggas."

Two thumbs up in Harlem meant that we had his stamp of approval. It meant the same thing in Chicago.

"Yo, dis is my man Bonkers. I don't fuck wit' no nigga on this earth like I do the god. Last time y'all came through to flex that move on them New Jersey niggas, Bonkers was in the bing doing a few months. Now, son is home and we eating and burping at the same time. Word to Harlem." He laughed. "Bonkers, this is Juelz and his right hand man TJ. Son n'em got mad hustle. We see two hundred thousand a week from the Windy fuckin' wit' kid n'em."

I shook up with Bonkers first. "Peace, shorty."

"Peace, god," he returned.

"What it do fool?" asked Juelz.

"Alive and getting it," Bonkers replied.

"Yo, I'm the head nigga on this Coke Kings shit, but my mans right here is slightly under me. When I ain't in the country, cuz a nigga love to fuck off in Dubai, son be running shit like a marathon sprinter, word up."

I laughed. That nigga Kammron had a way with words just like I did. I liked that. "Yo, so why was it so important that we touch down out here in NY?"

"Well, my mans just came home. The Coke Kings taking over the dope game. The muthafuckin' East Coast is ours, and we gotta do it big. I consider you niggas family, B. Word up. I'm celebrating my dude. I'm calling all the fam. Chicago is my second home, and when I think about Chicago, I think about you and Juelz. That ma'fucka belongs to you niggas, hands down." He hugged me. "Yo, we finna turn this bitch out tonight. We gon' start out in the hood, den move this bitch out to the Hamptons, where only the million dollar dope boys gon' be celebrating with the baddest of the bad bitches. Speaking of which, Dunn, who is that?"

Tonya stepped out of the Wraith and stretched her arms over her head. Her Fendi skirt was so tight that it showed off her ass, which was poked out like a sideways mountain. When she was done stretching, her tube top was still slightly raised. She had just a hint of gut, but when you was as thick as she was, it was impossible not to. She had a .380 in her hand as if it was normal. The sunlight reflected off of the chrome.

"That's my shorty. Her name is Tonya. She's Chiraq crazy." I told him.

"Word to the motherland, that Goddess is fine as a muthafucka. Introduce the Kid. All I need is an opening. I mean, unless you cuffing her like jeans that are too long." Kammron looked over to me.

I laughed. "It's good. I don't cuff nothing but blue face hunnits. Yo' Tonya, come here, shorty."

She pointed to herself, confirmed that I was talking to her, and then came over with her thighs juggling slightly. The closer she got, the more I could see the sunlight shining off of her Kylie Jenner lip gloss. She walked up and slid her arm around my waist. "What's good, daddy?"

"Kammron wanna meet you. He saw all of dem treasures from afar and he wanna see what it do." I nodded at Kammron. "That's him right there."

She frowned and looked over to him, and then up at me. "Yo, its gang gang all day every day. I belong to TJ. Ain't shit happening." She rolled her eyes and walked away from us with her ass jiggling.

"Whew-ee!" Kammron shook his head. "Yo, if I don't fuck shorty before you niggas leave on Monday, I'll send both of you hike with a hunnit racks apiece and two blocks in Harlem. Word to my mother Kathy."

I laughed again. "Bet those. Shorty's ass stubborn as hell. She's a Taurus just like me. Good luck wit' that, nigga."

***

We all bunched into an apartment building that Kammron had shut down. There were so many speakers blaring everywhere that it felt like the music was inside of my body. I eased through the crowd with two .45's in holsters. I was never able to get more than a few steps before one of the many Harlem goddesses was pulling on my wrist trying to shoot their shot. My neck was heavy with chains, and I was fitted in blue and white Prada with the matching Jordans.

One female in particular pulled my wrist as I was heading back into the hallway to find Juelz. I was a half foot out when I saw Kammron all up on Tonya spitting his best game. She eyed him through her Tom Ford lenses with a look that said he was trying too hard. The female pulled me into the kitchen and flipped her hair over her shoulders.

"I've been trying all night to get your attention. What, ole girl got you locked down or somethin'?" She was about 5'5" tall, light-skinned with piercing green eyes. Her hair was silky, and she was strapped. She smelled good too. Her lips were shining bright and juicy.

"Ain't nobody got me locked down, shorty. It's so many bad hoes in here I must ain't see you. That's yo' fault."

"My fault?" She looked offended, pointing to herself.

"That's what I said. It's plenty of boss niggas in here and you managed to peep me, right?"

"Yeah."

"Well, if you hadn't, that would have meant that I didn't take the time to think about crushing these niggas before I showed up, but I did, and you caught sight of me. The fact that you had to pull me by the wrist in order for me to see you means that you ain't hitting on shit. Don't touch me no more. You feel me?"

She touched her chest in shock. "Damn, it's like that?"

I adjusted my shades. "Bye, shorty." I eased past her and headed back into the party.

I scanned the crowd for Juelz. It smelled like weed, alcohol, cigarette smoke, and thick cups of Lean. I spotted Juelz dancing in the middle of two thick-ass Puerto Rican women and was about to make my way over to him when I felt my shirt being tugged. I turned around ready to snap out and came into view of Tonya. She looked angry.

"Daddy, I ain't feeling this party. Can we go back to the hotel? Please, this nigga Kammron is too overbearing and if he squeezes my ass again without my permission, I'ma blow his ass away, straight up." She laid on my chest. "Please rescue me. I don't want no nigga touching me but you."

I leaned down and kissed her forehead. "Awright, li'l baby. Let me holler at Juelz and we finna get up out of this bitch. Hold on."

As soon as I walked off, Kammron walked back up and started to holler at her again. I wanted to stop and check that nigga but I knew Tonya could handle herself. Instead, I walked up on Juelz. He was licking up and down one of the Puerto Rican's necks.

I tapped his shoulder. "Say, shorty, I'm about to take Tonya back to the telly, she ain't feeling dis scene."

"Yeah, well I am. Take her party-pooping ass on then. I'm tryna fuck both of these Harlem beauties, word to Cook

County." Cook County was the county that Chicago was located in. Every now and then me and Juelz said this whenever we were missing home.

"Awright, bruh, hit me up when you ready to go. I'll come scoop you so I can trail you."

"It's good, Blood. Yo, dis ain't my first time in Harlem. I know how to navigate these slums. I'll fuck wit' you in the morning. Peace, shorty."

I shrugged my shoulders and eased away from him. When I made it back to Tonya, she was snatching her wrist away from Kammron. She hurried to me and slid her arm around my waist. Kammron mugged her.

"Daddy, tell this nigga no means no. Damn, what the fuck is wrong with him?" I could tell she was fuming because she was shaking like how she got before she killed somebody out of anger.

Kammron walked up with a glass of Lean. He sipped from it. "That ain't how that deal goes, Blood. You can't be cock-blocking and expect me to pay my end of this bet. You gotta let me do me."

"What bet?" Tonya stood back and looked me over.

I lowered my head, and placed my hand over my forehead. "Here we go wit' down shit."

"Ain't no here we go. What bet did you make wit' dis out of town-ass nigga?" she snapped.

"Dat I could fuck before y'all left on Monday." Kammron snickered.

Tonya looked up at me as if she was hurt worse than she had ever been before. "TJ, drop me off at the airport right now, please. I don't give a fuck what you do wit' these New York niggas, but I need to be back home. I ain't built for this Apple shit." She made her way through the crowd toward the front door.

Kammron shrugged his shoulders. "I ain't know the hoes back in Chiraq were so sensitive. My bad." He grabbed the arm of another female that was strolling through and began talking to her.

T.J. Edwards

Chapter 10

When we got back to the hotel, Tonya rushed over and began to pack her clothes. "I can't believe you, TJ. You bring me all the way to New York just to front on me for these New Yorkers. After all you taught me and the crew about loyalty, I ain't seeing dat shit from you. Ugh. I'm so mad right now that I feel like busting you in your shit. That's on gang." She pulled her suitcase to her roughly and spilled most of the contents on the floor. Her greases, shampoos, combs, and pantyliners fell across the carpet. She took a deep breath and bent down to pick them up.

"I would never flex on you for no nigga. You my ma'fuckin' li'l shorty. That goofy-ass nigga made it seem like he could fuck you, and then when you gave his ass mo' attitude than what he used too he told me and Juelz that if he didn't fuck you by Monday that he was gon' give us a hunnit thousand apiece and a few blocks in Harlem."

"Dat all I'm worth to you is a few hunnit gees and some fuckin' land in Harlem? Wow." She picked up her suitcase from the floor and slammed it on the bed.

I eased up behind her and wrapped my arms around her small frame. "Li'l baby, daddy didn't even take the bet because I already know it's a fool's bet. I know how you get down, and I already know who dis pussy belongs to. You're daddy's baby girl, right?"

"I don't know."

I kissed her neck and bit into the skin. "I said right?" Now I was sucking on it.

She shuddered. "Right." Her eyes closed. She released her luggage and fell back into me. "Daddy, do you still love me like you said you did before?"

"Hell yeah I do, and I'd murder one of these New York niggas over you. You already know how I get down, that's on gang." I grabbed her tightly to me and bit into her neck hard enough to cause her pain.

"Oooh shit." She dug her nails into my thighs and became putty in my arms. "I love you too. You should know that I would kill for you with no hesitation. You're my ma'fuckin' daddy. You got me rolling a Benz and more money in my bank account than I've ever seen before. A bitch spoiled. That nigga can't just walk up and think that it's sweet. It's levels to dis shit. I'm used to being treated a certain way."

I lifted her Fendi dress and kissed down her spine. "What way is that, li'l baby?" When I got to her ass, I sucked on both cheeks and opened them. My tongue circled around her crinkle.

"Like a damn princess. You treat me good. Dat's why I play my role and pledge my loyalty to you, TJ."

I pushed her over the bed and spaced her thighs. I squatted behind her and kissed her cat through the thong lining before yanking it to the side. Her sex lips came out on display. They were dark caramel and puffy. I sucked first the right one and then the left.

"Dadddeee," she whimpered.

I locked my lips around her clitoris and went crazy on it. She started moaning at the top of her lungs, jumping back into my face. "You my daddy, TJ. You mine! Fuck New York! Fuck dese niggas!"

I slurped her juices hungrily, flicking my tongue at her clitoris until she came, pushing her luggage onto the floor. I picked her up. She wrapped her thick thighs around my waist. I fed her pussy juices to her, tonguing her down.

"You think daddy would trade on you? Huh, li'l baby?" I searched between us and slid into her deeply.

She tilted her head back. "Unh! Never!" she gasped.

I lifted her up and pulled her back down hard over and over, repeating the process. She dug her nails into my shoulder blades. I kept a tight grip on her, giving her the bidness. "Tell daddy...dat...you...love him." I slammed her harder and faster, moving her up and down.

"I love you! I love you! Aww fuck! I...love you." She leaned forward and sucked my face, licking all over it wildly.

I fell on the bed with me between her thighs. I was plowing like it was going to be my last time in the pussy. It kept on getting better and better the harder and deeper I went. She was so wet that it was running down my thighs all the way to my ankles. "I'm finna cum, shorty!"

Bam! Bam! Bam! Bam!

"Damn, this pussy good!" I groaned.

"Daddy, cum in me. Unh! Unh! Shit! Cum in me!" she screamed as she bit into my neck.

The feel of her pussy vibrating was too much for me. I dug deep and came hard, jerking between her thick thighs. I sucked her earlobes and all over her neck. I ripped her Fendi dress top down the middle and squeezed her titties together, sucking the hard nipples through the material.

When we finally finished, she climbed on top of me and rubbed all over my chest. Her little face rested in the crux of my neck.

"TJ, I know you told me that if me and you were ever going to get down that I would have to keep my feelings in check and stay in my lane, but I'm finding that hard. I ain't never had a real man in my life that treated me like you do. You make me feel special, and you take good care of me. I don't think I can keep screwing you and not develop some sort of feelings. I'm just being a thousand wit' you." She kissed my chest and ran her hand all over my stomach.

I gripped her fat ass and slid my hands down until I was cuffing her monkey. Tonya was strapped for being so young. She was also slightly bow-legged and now I understood why. "So what you saying, li'l baby?"

"I don't know what I'm saying because I love you. I like when we get together like this, but I always leave with so many feelings that it drives me crazy. Maybe it's because I'm still so young that I don't understand how I am supposed to shut off my emotions when it comes to you, but I just feel real shitty trying to do that. I wish we could just be together."

I sat up and pulled her off of me. She fell to my left. I stood up. "Yo, I already told you what it was when it came to that. You're the princess of our hood. I'm the king. I can love you, but we can't ever be together. Everything we do is business, even when we fuck. I pipe yo' ass down so that you can continue to stay focused on your tasks at hand, and not become under some other bum-ass nigga's spell. You gotta chase that bag, shorty. That's the only way you gon' be able to make it out of the ghetto and stay out. You're going where this fall?"

"To Clark University."

"To become what?"

"A child psychologist."

"Why?"

"Because I have to be the first one in my family to make it to and through college. I gotta break the mold."

"Why?"

"Because I am a strong black woman that can do anything I put my mind to." Her eyes teared up.

"What is the game?"

"A stepping stone. It's temporary, and I have to leave it when the fall classes start and you'll take over my tuition and school fees from there."

"Why?"

"Because you love me, and to love me means that I deserve more than the slums." She broke into full tears and rushed me, wrapping her arms around my neck. I picked her up. "I love you so much, TJ. I can't see myself being without you ever. Damn, you drive me crazy."

I held her while I planted kisses all over her face. "I love you too, and I got you. No matter what, I got you."

***

Juelz showed up at three that morning, beating on the hotel room door. When I opened it, I had a gun in my hand, and Tonya stood behind me with two .380s in hers. She had them aimed at him until we verified that it was actually him. Only then did she lower her weapons. Juelz brushed past me and punched his fist.

"Fuck wrong wit' you, bruh?" I asked him.

"Some bitch-ass nigga caught me slipping. I think one of those Rican hoes set me up." He punched his open fist again. "Damn!"

"What happened?" I asked. Tonya climbed back in the bed and pulled the sheets over her head.

"A nigga hit me for all of my jewelry and twenty thousand on my way out of the Harlem River Houses."

"The Harlem River Houses? What the fuck is that?" I wanted to know. What the hell was he doing around a river?

"They somethin' like row houses. Anyway, I was coming out to the whip to grab my box of condoms when the nigga laid me down and snatched my chain like I was a sucka or something. Fuck!" He swung at the air and nearly fell over. "Somebody gotta pay for that. That was three hunnit thousand in ice."

"What that fool Kammron say?" I started to get dressed.

"I ain't tell him shit. The nigga that did this shit had the audacity to do it without a mask too. I swear I'll never forget his ugly-ass mug. Bruh, we gotta roll out right now to see what we can find out."

Tonya pulled the covers from over her head. "Daddy, you want me to roll out wit' you?" She yawned and neglected to cover her mouth.

I waved her off. "Nawl, shorty, you good. Take ya ass to sleep because I'm waking you up at six in the morning so you can do a few of them online assignments. A'ight?"

She was mid yawn again. "O-kay." This time she covered her mouth with her hand. "I love you, and be safe."

"I love yo' li'l ass too, now get some rest."

***

Juelz leaned all the way back in the passenger's seat of the Wraith with his eyes low and red. He snickered and shook his head as if he'd discovered something amusing. "Yo, since when did you start telling that ghetto-ass bitch that you love her?"

I mugged him. "Why you always gotta disrespect my sistahs, bruh? Straight up?"

"Aw shit, here we go. Don't tell me that you're getting all soft over dese hoes. I thought you was born heartless, nigga."

"Man, answer my question? Why do you make it yo' bidness to always shit on the sistahs? I don't ever hear you talking that shit about those snow bunnies or them Spanish women, so what you got against sistahs?"

"I ain't got shit against them, I just don't fuck wit 'em like dat cuz they ain't bad enough. You telling these bitches that you love them and shit is ridiculous. Then I found out that you're using a lot of your trap money to pay for a few of them bitches to go to college. What the fuck is wrong wit' you?"

"Nigga, you can't tell me what to do wit' my money. Fuck. What, you think I'm just supposed to spend it all up on designer this and designer that? It's cool for me to invest in those racist-ass clothing designers, but I can't invest in the Black Queens of our hood? What type of shit is that?"

Juelz scratched his inner forearm and wiped his face with his right hand. "Man, you're investing in worthless hoes that ain't gon' never amount to nothing. That shit is stupid and pointless," he scoffed. "We out here trapping all fuckin' day so we can live good and do the shit that we wanna do. Foreign whips, trips, and exotic hoes. That's what it's about. It ain't about tricking yo' dick on buying a bitch an education. Hell, you ain't even got one." He laughed.

"Marie didn't either. Neither did my mother. That's why neither one of them had a chance. Them li'l sistahs might be out there trapping wit' us, but that ain't where their lives have to end. I see potential in them, and that's where I wanna spend my money. Fuck what you talking about. I love my Queens."

"That's cuz you stupid. Them bitches don't care about you or nobody else. When I was little, my pops had this black bitch turn him out on heroin real tough. She used to beat me so bad that twice I almost died. Not only did she introduce my pops to that shit, but my mother, too. She took both of them away from me and my life has been fucked up ever since.

Shid, the first time I ever got shot, it was because a black bitch set me up. In school, them hoes used to give me the bidness too, all because a nigga was a li'l bummy. They ain't never had no love for me, and I will never have no love for them." He sniffed and pulled on his nose.

I rolled for a few more blocks. "That's fucked up, shorty, I ain't know all of that. I'm sorry that you had to go through that."

"Man, fuck you, nigga I don't need yo' sympathy. I'm good. I've been slumping hoes wit' no mercy ever since I learned how to shoot straight."

"Yeah, well to me, my mother was the epitome of beauty, and so was my sister. I love my sistahs, and I'ma keep investing in them until I help as many as I can. Life is precious, and I don't know my death date, but as long as I'm here, I wanna make a difference."

"Whatever," Juelz grumbled. "You should run for president too, nigga. See if you can sew up the black vote.

"You'll be awright, wit' yo' tough ass."

He laughed. "Fuck you, nigga."

"Yo, I meant what I said by apologizing. I wish you would have told me about all of that earlier, I would have made sure that I was there to support you through it."

"What?" Juelz mugged me. "Yo, I swear to God, shorty, hanging around all of them hoes all of the time is making you soft. I don't need ya sympathies. I went through what I went through as a kid. It is what it is."

"You always gotta be so ma'fuckin' tough. Juelz, I'm your brother. You ain't gotta flex wit' me like you do everybody else. But it's good though, that's your struggle and I'ma let you have that." I kept pushing the Wraith trying to see what I could see."

We rolled into the Harlem River Houses neighborhood and it looked dirty and grimy. There were prostitutes walking up and down the block waving down cars or pulling up their already too short miniskirts. They smoked cigarettes and scratched their scalps while they sized up one car after the next. There were a few men out there as well, but none that looked like dope boys or Jack boys. I kept rolling, feeling like this was a blank mission.

"You know, TJ, whenever I get to feeling like I gotta shed those tears that only an animal can shed, that's when I make this cold-ass world feel my pain the most. I love killing niggas. It's the only thing that soothes my pain. That and fuckin' wit' as many foreign hoes as I can. I love money, too. It's something about being able to flex on a nigga that make me feel superior. Yo, I appreciate that love and worry you have for me, but I'm good. I'm strong. I'm from the Windy City, baby."

"Yeah, the Land. Awright den, bruh, long as you know that I got you, that's all that matters." I continued to scan the streets for the next five minutes. "Dawg, do you even know where this nigga live at?"

Juelz nodded. "To be honest wit' you, I don't even remember where the bitch stay. All dis shit look the same to me."

I was frustrated. "So what, we supposed to roll all around Harlem in areas that we don't know of, looking for a nigga who we don't even know either? How much sense does that make?"

Juelz nodded for a full minute. When he came back to, he scratched his inner forearm. "Damn, shorty, these Percs got a nigga all fucked up. I'm sleepy as hell. I might have to chop this shit up to the game."

"Or let that nigga Kammron know what happened in his city," I offered.

"Fuck that. I can't have that stain on my record. I'm renowned for murdering state to state. The Game finds out that a nigga snatched my chain and laid me down, my name gon' be tarnished. I can't have that. It's good, I'll see homie again.

Take me back to the telly." He leaned all the way back in his seat and closed his eyes.

"You sho'?"

"Yeah, that shit is small thangs to a giant." Minutes later, he was snoring like a bear.

Chapter 11

The next night was Kammron's big exclusive party. He'd found a way to shut down the city of New York and had called out only the elite members of the hip hop and dope game community. The event was being held at Illuminati's.

Illuminati's was one of New York's most prestigious high-end clubs that only the upper crust was able to get into. In order to be permitted, you had to have been given an invitation from the owner, and that was only at somebody like Kammron's request. The invitation came through your social media account with a series of numbers that translated your admittance and the number of people you were allowed to bring. I only needed a plus one because Juelz had been given his own invite. I chose to bring Tonya, my right hand woman while I was out here in New York.

We pulled up in front of the club with the Wraith freshly washed and waxed. The paint was hitting even in the night time. I stepped out of the driver's door fitted from head to toe in a blue and white Dior fit over the matching red bottomed number Five Jordans.

I had so many chains around my neck that I felt like one of those pit bulls in the hood. The gold was shining like a star on a clear night. Each wrist held a Patek, iced and chunky. The Chanel frames didn't have any medicine in them, but I was able to see clearly that I was supposed to be at this event holding my own. I felt and looked like a boss. I handed my keys to the valet and walked around to open Tonya's door.

She stepped out of the Wraith with her hair silky and full of sheen. The white and blue Dolce and Gabbana dress clung to her like a second skin. She was without a bra, and her nipples were hard and standing up like the erasers on a pencil. Her perfume was loud and alluring. Her dress was cut low enough to bring attention to the Louis Vuitton pumps that made her calves pop. Her toes were freshly pedicured. She was killing shit. She walked up to me and slid her arm inside of mine. "I'm nervous."

The paparazzi came and started to take picture after picture of us as we stepped onto the red carpet. I pulled her closer to me and held her possessively. "You ain't got shit to be nervous about. You are a young Queen. You deserve to be here. This is what it looks like when the family is starting to make noise throughout the country. I got you, do you hear me?" The cameras kept flashing.

"Yes, daddy. I love you." She smiled.

"I love you, too."

Kammron pulled up to the front of the club in a purple and black Rolls Royce Phantom. He had Juelz in the passenger's seat. They got out with four Puerto Rican girls from the back seat. Kammron had on a purple and black fur. His pants were Robert Cavalli, and he had so much jewelry around his neck that it was basically pointless. Juelz stood beside him just as iced. Both came and hugged me right away while the cameras flashed over and over again.

When we got into the club me, Tonya, Juelz, and his li'l Spanish dame headed to the Power Circle, which was a special section for VIP guests. I was handed two bottles of Moët, and Tonya was given a silver bowl full of orange Kush and a bottle of Cirôc.

We eased into the all-glass section and I got comfortable on the black leather couch that had good trimming. There was a stage the size of a pool table in the room. After we got seated, two exotic strippers came with robes and stepped up on the stage in front of us before they dropped their robes and began to dance nakedly to the Cardi B song coming out of the speakers.

Tonya mugged them. "Why they think we want to see these hoes naked? They could have kept that bullshit on." She rolled her eyes and finished twisting my blunt. She handed it to me.

I sparked that bitch and inhaled it deeply. I nodded my head up at the strippers and pulled out a knot of twenties, fifties, and hunnits. "Shorty, don't pay too much attention to what them hoes wearing or not wearing. Just enjoy this moment. You in dis ma'fucka wit' daddy. That's all dat matters." I put my arm around her and kissed her neck.

She grinned, and snuggled closer to me. "Damn, I love yo' thuggish ass."

I gave her a knot of cash. She threw a few bills on the stage. I turned up the bottle of Cirôc and held it to her lips so she could drink wit' me, then I drank from it again. I usually didn't like drinking after nobody, but we'd been kissing while we were in New York anyway. I just wanted to mentally escape through her, and so far it was working.

Juelz stood tossing five dollar bills at the strippers. His chains were double dutching, making a lot of noise. He drank from a bottle of Moët with a big smile on his face. "Say, TJ, dis dat shit that I'm talking about, shorty. We should have been doing shit like for Chicago. Ain't no way in hell we should have had to come all the way out here to New York for the Coke Kings to show us how it looks when a ma'fucka really gets money. We from the Windy City, baby. The murder capital. We were supposed to be inviting the Coke Kings down, not the other way around. We need a gangsta-ass name like they got, too. The Coke Kings. I like the sound of that." He threw another round of fifties and stopped to pop a handful of pills.

I kept my arm around Tonya. I could feel her shaking underneath me. There were so many exotic and beautiful women walking around wearing high fashion clothes and accessories that I imagined she had to feel out of place.

I didn't like her thinking like that. I leaned into her ear. "Hand to God, you're the baddest bitch in this room." I kissed her neck. "You come from the slums, li'l baby. All you know is the projects. But look at you. You're shining harder than these plastic hoes, and you're sitting next to a boss that loves you. Look at how these other bosses treat the women that they are with." I kissed her neck again.

She scanned the crowd. Her eyes were searching wildly. She shook her head after zooming in on something. Then she turned and looked into a few other sections before looking into my eyes. "That's why I love you so much, TJ. You know where I come from, and what I've been through, yet you still treat me like a Queen. How is a girl not supposed to fall in love with a man that does and acts like you do? It's so hard."

"Yo', long as you know I love you just as much. I just want better for you. I need you in the corporate world. I need you to break the mold because ain't none of this shit that I'm doing going to last. There is a time table on all of it. But with your brains and drive, man, li'l baby, the sky's the limit. I'ma have your back until you reach the top, too. I promise you that."

She was quiet for a minute. She lowered her head and wiped a tear from her eye. "Damn, I'm so crazy about you. I wish I was older, or that we could actually be together. I mean, I know we can't. I know that there are levels to all of this, and it's not my place to be your main or your wife and all of that, but damn I just need some part of you. Maybe I could be like your side wife or something."

I laughed and watched Juelz pick up a stripper before falling on the stage with her with him between her thick thighs grinding on her. "A side wife?"

"I guess I just made it up. But a side wife would be the female who you have a second life with. She knows about your main wife, and she's okay with it. She has your second home. She is your baby, and the one you come to when you need to escape from the pressures of your home life. She is free to roam, but more often than not she won't because she doesn't want any other filthy fuckin' man touching her. She is in love with you and only you, and she's content with being your safe haven. That's me. Can we at least think about giving me that slot? I mean, since I created it and all?"

I laughed and wrapped my arm more firmly around her. "Damn, yo' li'l ass'll make a nigga fall in love wit' you on some other shit. You're so adorable, and you're a killa like daddy. I'll tell you what, baby; If you can pass your first two semesters with passing grades, then we'll talk about that. Right now, I'm wit' you until the dirt. I ain't leaving you. You're my li'l woman. I just need for you to focus on you though, and nothing else. You hear me?"

"Yes, daddy." She laid her head on my shoulder. "You're perfect for me, TJ. You know how to treat me like a woman and a little girl at the same time. You're one hell of a man. Fuck these other niggas." She frowned and scooted closer to me.

Juelz was dancing with a stripper's legs wrapped around his body when he stopped. He walked her over to the couch and threw her down on it. Then he stood looking out of the glass windows with a mug on his face. "Bitch-ass nigga."

Kammron came into our section with his arm around Asian and Black twins. "Yo, Chiraq, y'all wanna flip these twins wit' me? They do shit to each other that they could be arrested for."

Juelz walked up to Kammron. "No disrespect, but I'm finna kill a nigga in yo' club." Juelz dug deep into his boxers and pulled out a .40 Glock. "Ain't no nigga gon' rob me and get away wit' it."

Chapter 12

Kammron wrapped his arm around the dark-skinned, heavy man's neck and continued to chat him up as they headed out of the back of the club. I walked behind them in silence. When they opened the door and stepped out into the dark and windy parking lot, both me and Tonya put some pep in our step.

Just as we got outside, I saw Kammron release his arm from the man's neck. He threw his arms up, confused. Juelz came out of the shadows with a mug on his face and his eyes cold as snow balls. The man paused and froze in place.

Juelz came off of his hip with his Glock. He cocked it. "Bitch-ass nigga, do you remember me?"

The man squinted his eyes, and then they got big. He threw his hands up. "Aw shit. Say, Money, that was all a misunderstanding. I got yo' shit right here." He had the nerve to be wearing all of Juelz's chains around his neck at one time.

Tonya closed the distance. She struck her. 380 to his neck. "Don't move, homie, or I'ma splash yo' shit all over the pavement." She slowly began to take Juelz's jewels off of the man's neck. The man was incredibly still and quiet. After she removed the last one, she slid them all into her purse and stepped back from him.

I stepped up and swung as hard as I could, rocking his bitch ass in the left eye socket. He twisted and fell to the ground, groaning in pain.

"Fuck wrong wit' you? This da Windy, fuck nigga." I kicked him in the ribs, flipping him over. My Jordan wound up on his throat. Blood seeped out of his left eye. He struggled to breathe.

"TJ, I wanna stank this nigga, shorty. Tell me I should stank this pussy, bruh, please," Juelz begged me.

I looked around. I didn't know where we were, and who could have possibly seen us. The last thing I wanted to do was to be locked up in a New York prison. I didn't know shit about their gangs or their hoods. I would have been lost. Even more than that, I couldn't have Tonya throwing her life away over some fuckin' jewelry. "Nawl, shorty, that nigga got what he got. We ain't gotta snuff him."

"What? But his punk ass robbed me. A Chicago god. Nawl, his bitch ass gotta feel this hot shit from the Blikka. I gotta do this for the land, if for nobody else. I can't go back home with this shit on my brain, word to Englewood."

"Fuck, yo', well let me remove Tonya from this situation. Come on, Goddess." I grabbed her wrist.

"Nawl, fuck that. This Chiraq all day. I'm riding for the fam. Kill that nigga, Juelz. Shit ain't sweet." She stood over the robber.

"Now you're talking." Juelz stood over him, ready to pull the trigger, when Kammron whipped an old Chevy Astro van into the parking lot. Bonkers jumped out of it with a red rag over his face. Two men came behind him and grabbed the robber from the ground while he kicked and hollered.

Kammron came and stood in front of Juelz. "Dawg, you should have told me what happened. I would have gotten yo' jewels back the same night, word to Harlem. Dis my borough." He mugged the robber. "Yo, kid, tell me what you want done to him and that shit is as good as done. Word up."

"I wanna murder his bitch ass. I wanna pop ten of these slugs into his face. I wanna make sure his bitch ass is dead. That's what I want." Juelz said this through clenched teeth.

"Say less." Kammron did a signal with his fingers. "We headed to the docks. Juelz, roll wit' me for a minute. TJ, you and your Earth can follow."

When we pulled up to the docks ten minutes later, the robber was pulled out of the van roughly. Bonkers slammed him to the ground and knelt to punch him in the jaw. "You ma'fuckas hitting the Coke King's guests. Bitch! That's a form of treason. Our niggas from the Chi got diplomatic immunity. You are going to be an example for all of the rest of yo' cutthroat, hard-headed idiots." He kept his Balenciaga on the robber's chest. "Handle yo' bidness, nigga."

Juelz stepped over him with no hesitation. He aimed his gun at his face. "Gang gang."

Boom! Boom! Boom! Boom!

***

That same night, I curled up in the bed with Tonya. We were lying on our sides, and I just wanted to listen to her heart. She pushed back into me, indicating that she wanted me to wrap my arms around her. I did. She moaned.

"What's on your mind, li'l baby?"

"I was just thinking about how crazy life is for all of us."

"What do you mean?" I kissed the back of her head.

"It's like we're supposed to be out here in New York celebrating and having a good time, but somehow, some way, it always winds up coming back to murder. It's like we can't go nowhere or do anything without the Angel of Death following us. That's just crazy to me."

"So, you don't think that Juelz should have killed that nigga that robbed him?"

"Hell yeah! Juelz is like your brother. Y'all are together all of the time. That was too close to home. If that would have happened to you, I would've murdered his punk ass too."

"He didn't have a choice then."

"Nawl, daddy, I know that, what I'm saying is that it doesn't seem to matter where we are, death and murder is always going to find us. What should be so different once I go off to Clark University? Who's to say that I won't have to buss my gun down there?"

"I hope you don't, but I also don't want you to be focused on no shit like that. Education needs to be the focal point."

She sighed. "I know. You make it seem like it is so easy and I really wish it was, but it isn't. Man, I'm finna miss Chicago, and especially you. I don't wanna imagine you having some other female laid up in my spot while I'm off trying to better myself. That would drive me crazy."

I snickered. "Yo' li'l ass jealous as hell. I like that, but yo' slot with me is solidified. Can't nobody park in yo' place. You're my li'l baby." I kissed the back of her head again.

"Are you sure?"

"Yeah, baby, I'm sure." I closed my eyes.

She grabbed my hand and placed it around her body. "Daddy, how old do you think we'll be when the Reaper comes to get us back for all of the wrong that we've done? Will we be in our thirties, or will we not even make it that far?"

"I don't know, li'l baby. We just gotta stay on guard every single day and watch each other's backs, knowing that each day could be our last. Daddy living in the moment. I can only control today. Tomorrow is going to be challenging enough. Are you done with all of your questions now?"

"Just one more. You know how you were saying that if I did well in school that you would consider me as being your side wife all of that?"

"Yeah, baby, I remember, what about that?" I was getting sleepy.

"Well, what if I did good in school and then you made me your main wife? I wouldn't mind you having a side piece or whatever as long as you only went over there when we weren't jamming the way we are supposed to. But I would make sure that we were always on the best of terms because I love you."

"And because I love you, I would never allow for you to settle for either a second slot, or a spot where a man is trying to force you to share his loyalty. If a man truly loves a woman, then all he'd need is her. If a man tells you that he needs more than just you, then he isn't your one, and you should never sacrifice yourself, or your dignity, for him. Baby, because I love you, and I know what you deserve, I would never marry you or ask you to be my side wife. You are too precious for that. You're my li'l baby."

"But I wanna be more than that. Damn, why can't I make the rules?" She rolled over until she was facing me. "I wish we were married. I know you would never cheat on me and you would spoil me to death. Ain't no man ever treated me like you, TJ. You are my whole heart, and I'm going to go crazy when I leave for school this fall." She kissed my lips and licked all over them. "Don't nobody do me like my daddy do." She sucked my top lip and then the bottom one, holding each longer the other.

Then she climbed on top of me and pulled my dick out. She laid with her chest on mine, reached behind herself, and slid me into her tight hot pocket. Her eyes rolled into the back of her head. "Mmm, I love my daddy." She bounced up and down slowly at first, gradually picking up speed while I held her waist. In only a few minutes, she was bouncing higher and higher, screaming at the top of her lungs.

I laid back and allowed for her to ride me until she came hard. She shuddered and fell forward, biting into my neck. I slammed her middle down hard onto me over and over. "This daddy pussy. This daddy's." I growled, humping up from the bed. Her box was extra hot and wet. It felt so good that I began to groan with each stroke. I looked between our sexing bodies and saw that she had my piece glistening from her juices.

"Daddy. Daddy. I love you. I love you, daddy. Only you." She slammed herself down with velocity and came screaming at the top of her lungs. Tears came down her cheeks.

I rolled her over and got between her thighs, inserted myself, and slow stroked her li'l pussy while I sucked all over her neck. She wrapped her ankles around my waist and her wrists around my neck, moaning.

"You're my baby. I love you, girl. I love you. Only daddy. Only daddy." Deeper and deeper. My teeth dug into the flesh of her throat. She shuddered and came again, crying harder. "Daddy ain't going nowhere. I got you. I promise. You hear me?"

"Yes, daddy. Yesssss! Shit yes!" Her eyes rolled into the back of her head. She arched her back with her mouth wide open.

I licked all around the rim of her lips. My tongue touched hers. I sped up the pace. My strokes became longer and deeper. When I got ready to cum, I was sucking her hard nipples. I fucked as fast and hard as I could while she dug her nails into my shoulder blades. Then I came deep within her before pulling out and cumming all over her thick hairless pussy lips.

***

I woke up early the next morning to Juelz beating on the hotel room door. After he explained to me what he wanted, we wound up sitting inside of his hotel room with both Kammron and Bonkers there on the couch across from us. Juelz rubbed his hands together with a Disneyland smile on his face.

"Awright, my nigga here now, tell us what y'all are trying to do?"

Kammron slid to the edge of his couch. "What it do, TJ? Look, we were telling ya mans that we wanna venture out to Chicago wit' this coke and smack. Kid, we got a stupid plug across the waters and New York is already flooded along with a few other choice regions out east here. Anyway, we wanna dump some major shit off down in the Windy City and have you li'l niggas rock that shit. What do you think?"

The first thing that came to my mind was that these New York niggas was trying to make workers out of us. "So y'all meaning that we cop from you two and we do our own thing, or what?"

Bonkers shook his head. "Nawl, Blood, we wanna front you niggas like twenty Eagles a piece. That's forty right there. Y'all will move them for us, and we'll lay you a made price for every brick moved. You can also buy yo' shit from us separately and do your own thing, too. We won't knock your hustle."

"Why wouldn't we just buy the shit flat out and hustle for ourselves? The way you're saying it is we will always be indebted to the Coke Kings. I don't like owing no nigga shit." I mugged both Kammron and Bonkers. The worst time to fuck wit' me was when I first woke up. I was extremely irritable at that time.

Kammron shook his head. "We ain't thinking about no debt. We're thinking about expanding. I mean, unless y'all are cool with us moving a few of our branches down there and us opening up shop from here. I wouldn't mind paying for your G passes and security once a week at a base price. On top of that, you could still cop a heavy shipment from us biweekly

for the low. I'm talking about pure quality, A-1 boy and girl."
In Chicago and New York, dope boys often referred to Girl as
cocaine and Boy as heroin. That was dope talk.

Juelz looked me over. "What if we gotta crush a few decks
before we make this merger shit happen? Y'all gon' send
some hittas down to the Land to make this happen?"

Bonkers frowned. "You muthafuckin' right."

Juelz rubbed his chin. "That's interesting. What you think,
TJ?"

"Ain't no room on the North side. I got that shit locked
down. Whatever you do with the west and south east, that's
on you. But whatever ground we give up in Chicago, they
gotta give up equally out here in New York. If we gon' eat,
then all of us are going to burp, it's as simple as that." I stood
up. "I'm tired as a bitch. Y'all let me know what you come up
wit' and we'll shake on it. Juelz, I trust you to be smart." He
stood up and I gave him a half of a hug.

"I got this," he promised.

Eight hours later I was on a flight back to Chicago with a
big-ass smile on my face. I missed my homeland. I couldn't
wait to see the buildings, the el train, and my slums. In my
opinion, there was no place on Earth like the Windy City.

Chapter 13

The next day, after I got back from New York, Punkin showed up at my two-bedroom house with my son in her arms. I was already on my way out of the house to do a little grocery shopping at Walmart when I opened the door and saw her bouncing him up and down on her hip. He had on a red and black Polo outfit with the matching LeBron's. When I opened the door, she smiled up at me.

"Look who I got here with me. Somebody wanna see their old man, ain't that right, li'l TJ?"

I took him out of her arms and kissed his chubby cheeks. He smiled and hugged me tight. I could tell that he was going to be strong like me. "What brings you over here unannounced?"

"Unannounced?" She rolled her eyes. "Boy, I got your son with me, ain't no such thing as me being unannounced." She held up five fingers and blocked my face with them, walking into my crib. "Who do you got over here?"

"Shorty, you betta take them nasty-ass shoes off in my house. You know I don't play that," I snapped, closing the door with my hip.

She paused and began to take them off. "Aw, so you can walk all through my house wit' yo' funky shoes, but when I come to your pad, I gotta take mine off. What type of foolishness is that?"

I sat on the couch and made Junior stand in front of me. I looked him over from head to toe. "Yo, why my son got all these scratches on his face? What have you been doing to him?"

She came into the living room and sat across from me. "I ain't did nothing to him. He did that to himself. Why would you even ask me somethin' that stupid anyway?"

Here we go. Punkin wanted to argue, I could feel it. "Punkin, what's up? Why are you here?"

She curled her upper lip. "Why am I here? When you start trying to treat me like I'm one of your other thots in the ghetto? You better check yourself, TJ."

Damn, she was getting on my nerves already. "Why are you here?" I was louder now, and I became furious.

"You haven't seen him in a little while, and I figured that you would want to. Excuse me for trying to do the right thing." She crossed her thighs.

Her skirt fell backward, exposing the underside of her caramel thighs, but I didn't care. After spending so much time with Tonya, she had my mind transformed to a feeling that Punkin had never given me. It was a feeling of love and need. I felt none of these things when it came to Punkin, only irritation and anger. I didn't like arguing with nobody. Arguing often led to murder for me.

"Awright, well, let me spend some time with him then and I'll get him back to you in a day or so. How does that sound?"

"That sounds stupid. Why can't we get used to spending time together as a family? I mean, that is what we are going to be once we finally leave Chicago together, aren't we?"

I frowned at her. "Leave Chicago? When are we supposed to be doing this?"

She smacked her lips. "I knew it. You just be saying shit to hear yourself talk. Now you don't remember saying we were going to leave Chicago together so we could be a family with our son?"

"Nawl, I don't remember that. I wouldn't even know where to go. Chicago is my homeland. Always has been, always will be. Anything that takes place in this life, it can happen right here in the Windy."

She stood up and pressed her fingers to her temples. "Damn, I knew I was fuckin' up getting involved with you." She walked off for a second and then looked back at me. "What are your plans for our family, TJ? Huh? Don't you realize that now that we have a son, you have to have a set plan for our lives? Look at that little boy."

I picked Junior up and kissed his lips. "What you on, shorty? What, you felt like arguing so you brought yo' ass all the way over here to the Northside so you could pick wit' me, dat it?"

"I ain't picking wit' you. You picking wit' yo' damn self. You're always trying to find a way to wiggle out of something. I need to know what your fuckin' plan is for us!" Junior started to scream and cry.

I glared at Punkin. I stood up with my son, rubbing his back. "I thought you said it wasn't healthy for either of us to be cursing in front of him."

"Whatever. What are your plans?"

I shrugged my shoulders. "I'ma keep hustling and running up a bag for my son. I just opened a trust for him. It's at nine thousand dollars, and I'ma do nine a month until I ain't able to do it no more. I got one of my old school homies that runs a few businesses to wash the dollars for me so it'll come back clean. He writes the checks for nine thousand a month, and I'll pay him ten. For now, that's the best I got."

"So our son ain't even a year old and already you got him involved in a money laundering scheme? Wow." She opened her hands. "Gimme my baby."

Junior was already crying. I took a step back out of her reach and tried to calm myself down. "Damn, Punkin. You got niggas out here that ain't trying to nothing for their children. All they do is hustle and spend all of their cash on themselves, yet here I am honestly trying to make it happen for mine and you don't give me no credit. That shit is irritating." Junior was kicking and screaming so badly that I handed him to her. I was over it. Clearly he preferred her over me.

Punkin rested her lips on his cheek and bounced him slightly. "It's okay, baby. It's okay, Mommy is right here." She hummed a tune that I didn't know where it came from. He began to cool out, then she popped a pacifier into his mouth. "It's not that I don't give you any credit, TJ, I just expect more from you. You're an intelligent man, and you could have so much more if you just applied yourself. Your problem is that you are okay with living in and dying in the streets. You feel like you already know your final chapters, so why even try? That's what I hate about you."

"And what I hate about yo' bougie ass is that you act like you're too good to spend these blue faces that come from the trap. I run into so many struggling single mothers in the ghetto that feel relieved when I put a few G's in their hands so they can pay their bills and shit. They don't give a fuck how I got the money as long as they ain't getting evicted at the end of every month."

"Yeah, and that's because those bitches deserve to live in the ghetto. They ain't never been nothing, and they will never amount to anything. That's how I feel, and that's just what it is."

I felt like I wanted to puke in her face. "You really think you're better than them sistahs in the hood, don't you? Why, 'cause yo' people left you with a li'l money? Dat makes you better than them?"

She shrugged her shoulders. "Your words, not mine."

I scoffed. "Shorty, where I come from, a ma'fucka'll take that li'l weak-ass bag you got put up and feed it to their wolves. You ain't better than nobody because you found a way out of the slums. Yo' ass should be the main one trying to help the sistahs back in the trenches. Yo' family history ain't no mystery," I spat, walking into her face.

"What do you mean by that?" She cuffed the back of Junior's head as his eyes closed and he proceeded to doze off.

"Like you didn't know that yo' pops used to sell dope in Englewood. Yo' mother sold pussy for a li'l while until she ran into yo' pops. That nigga pulled her out the trenches when he fell in love. He's the reason you got the bag that you do now, because before he got killed, he was doing the same thing that I'm doing for Junior with putting him up a trust fund. So don't judge me when your roots are a mirror to my own. Don't judge those Queens in the hood because if your father wasn't responsible like I'm trying to be, yo' ass would be them." I walked off on her and left her looking stupid in the living room. When I made it to the kitchen, I grabbed an apple juice and drank some of it. She always managed to piss me off.

Punkin came into the kitchen ten minutes later. At that time, I was checking the NBA scores on my phone to see what my favorite basketball player LeBron was doing.

She stopped beside my chair and placed her hand on my shoulder. "Can we start over?"

"How do we do that?" I scrolled down the stats and nodded my head. My dude was still a beast.

"Look, TJ, I like you. You used to like me real tough. I mean, you pursued me all through high school. Somehow or some way, our signals have gotten crossed and along our individual journeys, we've lost sight of one another. We have a son together, and he needs the both of us. How can we start from scratch so that this time we can do this right?"

"Damn, shorty, I don't know. It seems like every time you and I come together, we are arguing about somethin'. I mean, I wish I could see you in the same light that I used to see you back in high school, but the truth is, I don't. I think I'm maturing in a different direction."

She looked hurt. "Okay, but how can you use the words mature and different direction when it comes to me and your son? If you are turning away from us, then you aren't maturing. You're just turning into a ghetto punk like the rest of those dope boys in the inner city of Chicago, and how couldn't you? Sooner or later, a man always becomes what his heart lusts after. You lust after money, drugs, fast women, and murder. That's why we argue so much, because you are a fuckin' thug."

I ran my fingers through my dreads. "Yo, I don't wanna be with you, Punkin. I'll cash you out on the strength of Junior, but you are too extra. You get on my damn nerves too much, and you don't make me feel good."

"You, you, you, you. That's all you speak and care about is you. Damn, you need to grow the fuck up. The minute that li'l boy was born, it was no longer about you anymore. It became all about him."

"That shit goes both ways though. It ain't about just you no more neither. You are trying to set things up so that they benefit you in a way that you deem perfection. If it ain't your way, then it's the wrong way. That shit ain't cool either. I don't think we jam. I ain't feeling you, and that's just that. I wanna take care of my son. You and I don't need to have any form of a relationship outside of parenting."

She pointed her finger in my face. "Nigga, I done did too much shit to not get what I want out of yo' ass. You gon' respect me and you're going to be with me in the way that I say. That's just that. We got a son."

I smacked her finger out of my face and grabbed her by her neck, carrying her across the kitchen until she was slammed into the wall. "Keep yo' fuckin' fingers out my face before I break them bitches. You ain't gotta talk wit' ya digits. You feel me?" I let her go.

She swung and busted my nose. My shit got to leaking right away all over my Gucci shirt. "Don't you ever put yo' hands on me. You don't own me, TJ. I will kill yo' punk ass. You don't know who you dealing wit'. Trust me on that." She pushed me backward.

I stumbled and caught my balance. I shot forward and slapped her across the face, then grabbed her by the neck, lifting her off of her feet with one hand. "Bitch, you got me fucked up." Her feet kicked and dangled while she choked. I dropped her, and she fell to her knees crying. My nose got worse because of my adrenalin.

"You didn't do Sodi like this. You treated that Spanish bitch like a Queen. I hated her, and I hate you!" she shouted. She climbed to her feet and left the kitchen.

I grabbed a towel and tilted my head backward after spitting blood into the kitchen sink. I was fuming. It took me twenty minutes to get my stuff to stop bleeding. That's when my doorbell rang.

When I got to the front of the house, Punkin was letting Reggie into it. He rushed inside with two other dudes. They ran across the living room and into the kitchen toward me. I flipped the table. The first one that got close, I rocked his ass with a left hook, knocking him out cold. Then came the second one. I kicked the chair in his path and stepped on it, kneeing him directly in the nose, feeling it break. He fell backward and tried to rush me again. Two hard punches sent him to the floor next to his homie.

Reggie stopped in his tracks. "Why the fuck you put your hands on Punkin?"

I was breathing hard. I could still taste my blood in the back of my throat. "Fuck you doing in my house, nigga? Huh?"

He lunged forward and swung a haymaker, missing me. His momentum sent him all off balance. I dove and tackled him into the sink. We wound up on the floor tussling. He was strong. I head-butted him in the face. He groaned out loud with blood running down his face.

I flipped him over and straddled him. As soon as I had him pinned, I rained down blow after blow rocking his goofy ass. Blood spurted under my fists. His eyes crossed. I punched him some more. It felt good. I wanted to finish him right on that kitchen floor.

"Get off of him!"

Bam!

I grew dizzy and fell sideways. I looked up at Punkin, who was holding a skillet in her hand. She lifted it over her head, ready to swing it again. I fainted as soon as I felt it crash into my skull.

Chapter 14

I was laid up in the hospital for two days. I got a few staples, and they wanted to monitor my brain activity to make sure that the pan hadn't knocked me stupid. They ran a few tests and then let me go. Instead of going back to Chicago, I stayed in a motel in Kankakee, Illinois.

I couldn't be in Chicago. I knew that if I was that there was no way around me not killing Punkin, and since she was the mother of my child, I had to restrain myself and use some common sense. So I stayed in Kankakee until I was able to gain some perspective. I still couldn't believe that she would go against me and attack me for her cousin. I was her child's father, so by hierarchy, she was supposed to ride with me over him- at least, that was what I thought. But it was what it was.

I stayed in the motel and smoked Kush blunt after Kush blunt until I got so high that all I could do was pass out to sleep. This wound up happening for two weeks straight. By that time, the staples were ready to be removed and I was tired of calling shots to my troops from outside of Chicago. I wanted to go home.

The morning that I was set to return to Chicago, Jelissa hit me up early in the morning. "TJ, are you awake?" she texted.

"Yeah," I wrote, "what's good?"

"Pick up the phone." The next thing I knew, my phone buzzed.

I picked it up and placed it to my ear. "Hello?"

"Hey, what have you been up to? Have you forgotten about me?"

I sat up, and rubbed my eyes with the back of my hand. "Nawl, shorty, what's good?"

"Nothing. Deion wound up giving me Rae'Jon back. My mother hit him up and they did the exchange over in Newark,

New Jersey where I'm from. He got my youngest son right now and I'm so sad that I need to get away. I need you to come somewhere with me."

I felt like shit because a part of me had forgotten about her situation. I had been so consumed with my own that hers had slipped my mind. "Damn, Jelissa, I'm sorry. I'm slipping. Where do you need me to go? What, you tryna get A'Jhani back?"

She sighed into the phone. "Nawl, I don't feel like all of that drama in my life right now. I wanna get away. Question for you: have you ever been skiing before?"

I laughed. "Skiing? Man, stop playing wit' me. Ain't that some white people's shit?"

She was quiet. I could tell that she was a little thrown off. "It's anybody's thing that wants to do it. I don't think it belongs to any color."

Now I felt stupid. "Yo, why are you asking me if I wanna go skiing?"

"Because I want you to fly away to Colorado with me. I got a timeshare over in Aspen and I want you to go with me so that we can get an understanding with each other. I mean, you still plan on pursuing me, right?"

I took a second. I couldn't help but to imagine Deion and the whole A'Jhani situation. That seemed like a lost cause. How could I ever be with a woman who had given birth to my brother's seed? That just seemed so wrong, yet I wasn't clearly sold on not pursuing her.

The energy whenever we were in the same room just took me to another place in time. Then I thought about Punkin. I still couldn't believe that she had turned on me for Reggie. That had me vexed. When my li'l baby Tonya crossed my mind, I wanted to turn Jelissa down and call my li'l shorty up.

I needed to hear her call me daddy and act all possessive over me. That shit low key drove me nuts.

"Dang, okay, I guess I got my answer."

"Nawl, it ain't nothing bogus. You know what, Jelissa? I think that we, as grown adults, need to take the time to get to know each other and to get an understanding with one another. I'm all in like a good poker hand. When do we leave?"

"You had me scared there for a minute. We leave tomorrow and we come back on Monday, so get all of your affairs in order. And TJ?"

"What's good, shorty?" My throat was dry as hell.

"Thank you for coming. I appreciate you."

"You're welcome."

"Okay." She hung up the phone.

I spent the entire day in Chicago picking up money and dropping off work to a few of my buildings and traps on the north side. When the orders were given, I bounced to another side of the trenches and did the same thing all over again. My security was in place. My safe houses were stacked. Juelz was left in charge, and by early the following day, I had my suitcase, ready to bounce.

***

When we stepped on to the plane, I would be lying if I didn't say that I was nervous. I had never been on a plane but one time before, and I was terrified of heights. I started thinking about 9/11 and all kinds of plane crashes. The interior of the Delta was small and compact. I felt like I couldn't breathe and there were so many people already on the plane that I worried about it being at capacity. There was no way that a plane was supposed to hold that many people, I thought.

It really blew my mind when I was sure that we were getting ready to sit in first class on some boss shit, but Jelissa walked me all the way to the back where the coach seats were. Even though I had never been on a plane before, I knew that first class meant reserved for bosses, and coach meant that yo' ass was hurting. Since I was hood rich, I wasn't wit' that coach shit. I grabbed her wrist before we made it through the coach curtains.

"Say, Jelissa, if you're having money troubles or whatever, I don't mind paying for the tickets just to make sure that we fly in style. I ain't wit' sitting in those broke nigga seats. I got stupid cash. What the bidness?"

She frowned. "I am more than capable of paying for first class seats for the both of us, but I don't mind coach. It keeps me humble, and besides, all we're missing is a little peanuts and champagne. Trust me, they ain't got Moët. That's what you drink, right?"

I had to laugh at that. "Yeah."

A dark-skinned flight attendant came and stopped in front of us. "Excuse me, but you two will have to take your seats and put on your seat belts. We are set to take flight in a matter of minutes. Thank you." She walked off and gave the same orders to a few more people.

I gave in and followed Jelissa to our seats, which were way in the back just before the bathrooms. She allowed for me to slide in. I went ahead. She stored her few items in the storage area above our heads, and then she was sitting beside me. She smelled good. She always did.

"You okay, Mr. First Class Man?" She snickered.

The plane began to roll. I had my window shade open. I watched us gaining speed on the runway. My stomach began to get butterflies inside of it. "I'm good. Well, actually, I'm feeling a li'l sick because I ain't never been in a plane other than one time before. I don't really fuck wit' heights."

"Well, do you wanna pray before we take off? We gotta hurry up."

I wanted to act all tough and shit, but I decided against that. My mother had always stressed to me the power of prayer. "Yeah, shorty, say a prayer for us."

"Okay." She grabbed my big hands and placed hers over them. "Father, in the mighty name of Jesus, we come to you humbly and most submissive. We pray under the blood of Christ, and in His holy name. We ask that you protect us during this flight. Please place our angels on high alert, and please continue to be with us. We are fearful, but we have faith. We are in Your hands, Father. In the mighty name of Jesus we pray. Amen."

"Amen," I repeated. I felt better. I was still scared as a kid about to get a whoopin', but I was better than I was.

When the plane jerked and lifted into the air, I thought I was going to lose my mind. I closed my eyes and thought about everybody back in Chicago. Then I thought about my mother Deborah and my sister Marie. I grew solemn. I missed them. Suddenly death didn't scare me so much. I felt like whatever happened on the plane, it happened. I couldn't change it and to be honest, I didn't know if I really wanted to.

Jelissa placed her hand on top of mine. "I still can't believe that you agreed to come with me. It really does mean a lot. I already know how important you are to the slums. I know that time is money, so the fact that you were willing to set all of that aside just so you could be here with me is so amazing. I really am thankful." She smiled and looked so fine to me.

"Thank you for inviting me, especially after I dropped the ball on the whole helping you track down Deion thing. I got sidetracked. You know how the streets are."

"Yeah, I do, and it's okay. It wasn't your baggage to begin with." She looked down the aisle and I could tell that she was uncomfortable.

"So what made your mother decide to do the transaction?"

She shrugged her shoulders. "I don't know. I gave her all sides to the story, and she gave me her honest opinion. She didn't think that it was fair for me to hold out on Deion with A'Jhani, especially if I didn't even know if I wanted him or not. She thought that it was only right for the father to have a chance to bond with his child. She doesn't like Deion or his ways, but what's right is right. Yvonne is not about games. That's my mother's name, in case you didn't pick that up."

"I did." Now the plane was in the air and the pilot was saying something about how it was okay to move about the plane and to screw wit' the electronics. "So how are you feeling?"

"I don't know. I guess when it comes to Deion, I always feel like he is winning or getting over on me. He seems to have this thing where he can do anything he wants and never has to answer to anybody. It's very irritating and overwhelming. There are just no wins when it comes to him. I feel trapped, and a part of me just wants to let him have A'Jhani, but then that mother part of me wants to fight. I am stuck between a rock and a hard place. I don't wanna deal with him ever again but this child has me locked in for the next seventeen plus years. I'm so lost and weary that I just needed a vacation."

"Where is Rae'Jon right now?"

"He's with my mother. She's back home at her house in Chicago. She will have him for a week and then his sperm donor gets to have him for a few days. I swear to you, my life is in turmoil. I wish I was still a virgin."

"I understand that. That seems like you're going through a lot."

"I am, and you're telling me that you still wanna get involved with me? There is so much more than what meets this pretty face. I come with a lot of baggage. I am a damn good woman. I am loyal. God-fearing. Honest, devoted, and sexually open. But underneath all of that, it takes work to be with me. Work and countless hours of sacrifices. I am a full-time job, and so are my children. You can't just have me without these struggles, TJ. This is one thing that I need you to know."

I laid my head back on my seat and tried to make sense of everything that she was telling me. It seemed like a lot, and I honestly didn't know if I was ready for all of that as much as I wanted to be. I was already feeling some type of way about Deion. I hadn't gotta the chance to catch him, but I knew that when I did, I was going to take his breath away permanently.

Then it hit me. If Deion currently had A'Jhani right now, then it wouldn't be nothing for me to find out where he was laying his head. Jelissa seemed like she wanted to get rid of him just as much as I wanted to punish him. All I had to do was find a way to get the information up out of her. I would be able to find out where he was, and then I could finish him. Hell yeah. I smiled on some evil shit.

"So what happened between you and Punkin?"

"What are you talking about?"

"I heard some things, plus I'm friends with her on Facebook. What did she hit you with a pan for?"

I got angry instantly. "Yo', she put that shit on Facebook?" I was in disbelief.

"Yeah, what happened?"

"Man, that broad is a thorn in my side. I was whooping her cousin and she wound up blindsiding me with a pan. She's lucky she did too because I was finna body his weak ass."

"Damn, that's bogus. How she gon' choose her cousin over her child's father? Then to hurt you like that... That doesn't even make sense."

"It's all good. I'ma catch dude's ass and when I do, it's curtains." I was seething. "You know what? I don't even wanna talk about that shit right now. Let's change the subject. Matter of fact, I've been up since early this morning. I'm finna snooze for a minute. I'll talk to you when I wake up.

"Awright, dang."

We didn't say another word to each other until the plane landed. Even then it was awkward. I was sure that our little vacation time was going to be strained.

I missed Tonya, as much as I hated to admit that. I never argued with her, and she was always dead set on giving me as much love as possible. Even though a man could be heartless in the streets, when it all came down to it, there was always a part of him that yearned for a female to be the way Tonya was to me. It made me feel wanted, appreciated, and most of all, like I meant something. She captivated my every thought until we touched down in Aspen, Colorado.

Chapter 15

I had never seen so much snow in one place and at one time in all of my life, nor had I ever seen mountains before. That was a little trippy to me. Jelissa had a timeshare at Shadow Mountain, where there were large wooden cabins strategically placed all around. We stepped inside the one that was supposed to be the one we were staying at, and I was taken aback by how cozy it looked.

It was huge on the inside. Everything seemed as if it was made of wood. There was a huge roaring fireplace with a small bear-like rug in front of it. Above the fireplace was a picture of a black Jesus hanging on the cross. There were a series of paintings that ranged from Michelle Obama to Condoleezza Rice. It smelled good, and I could see myself chilling here for a few days. I dropped our suitcases. Then my eyes shot forward and I saw that there was no television. I felt about ready to panic.

Jelissa started to tidy up the place with familiarity. She moved about setting things in a way that made her feel more comfortable. When she finished, she picked up her suitcase and waved for me to follow her.

"Come on, Mr. First Class." She laughed.

I walked behind her, irritated that her coat hung so low that I couldn't see her li'l plump ass underneath it. We walked down a long hallway and stopped abruptly. She turned a gold knob on a door and pushed it inward. We stepped into a room that had a big bed inside of it. There was another crucifix nailed on top of this one. The covers were burgundy and looked as if they were silk.

"Okay, you can set your suitcase down right here. There is a dresser over there, and the closet is full of hangers. The bed is new and is a Sealy Posturepedic. You're good to go."

She began to make her way out of the room with her suitcase still in hand.

"Wait a minute, shorty, if I'm sleeping right here, then where the hell are you sleeping?"

"In the other room. There is a bed and all of that in there. Why, what's the matter?"

I dropped my stuff, and slid into her face taking a hold of her hips. "Yo, I know you ain't brought me all the way from Chicago here to Aspen just so we could sleep in separate beds? What type of shit is that?"

She looked up at me and set her suitcase on the carpet. "Well, what were you expecting?"

"For us to get acquainted. Come on now." I pulled her to me and rubbed my hands all over her ass, cuffing the cheeks. She was strapped back there. I loved her slim frame that was so misleading when it came to all of that ass.

She removed my hands from her backside and looked into my eyes. "TJ, I already told you that I need to make sure that you can handle my situation before we move forward in any way. I also need to know what you plan on doing in your own life. Sex is one thing, but after we finish doing the do that only takes under an hour, we're going to seriously have to figure out where we are going to go with things." She eased out of my embrace.

I was salty. "Yo', had I known we were going to come down here for all of this, I would have turned yo' ass down. I swear I had a completely different idea of what we were about to be doing." I kicked my suitcase out of my way and jumped backward on the bed, lying with my back on it and my arms crossed in front of my chest.

Jelissa laughed. "Boy, you look like a big-ass pouting kid. You betta stop all of that." She laughed some more.

I didn't see anything funny. I felt like I was losing time and money for no reason. Besides all of that, I hadn't gotten any pussy since me and Tonya had been in New York weeks ago. I was feening, and Jelissa was looking good as a buffet to a fat man. "Yo, it's all good. Gon' 'head and set yo' shit up den. I'ma lean back and catch some Z's," I lied. I was already planning on calling Tonya and having her buss that kitty open for me while we did a Facebook video. I needed to see those goods so I could get one out. Long as I was able to rub one out real quick, I would be good. I was sure of that.

"Well, you ain't gotta automatically write the trip off as a bust. I got some cool things planned for us to do."

"Does any of them involve me seeing you naked? Please tell me that."

She laughed again, showing off her dimples. "Everything ain't about sex, TJ. You have to be able to see past that at least for a minute. How about this. We are here for three days, right, not counting today?"

"Yeah."

"Awright. If you can give me three of the four days that we are going to be here, I will give you the last one, and we can do whatever you wanna do. How about that?"

I sat up, and looked her up and down. All I kept on thinking about was that sexy-ass caramel body. Her 'fit was snug, and the way she moaned in my ear drove me crazy. I had to have her. "Awright, that's a bet. But the last day is mine, right?"

"Right."

"Well, let's get it started. What do you wanna do first?"

A smile came across her face. "Get up, Mr. First Class, you are about to have the time of your life."

***

I couldn't believe that I was doing this just so I could get her ass back in the bed. That was the only thought going through my mind as I stood up on the skis. The wind was blowing harshly. Snow came from the sky in thick patches and I was colder than a polar bear's living room. I held both poles in the snow and slowly allowed for myself to come to the hill that Jelissa was trying to get me to ski down. When I got to the apex. I swallowed my spit and I was sure that this was how I was going to die.

Jelissa came up skiing like a veteran from the cabin. She stopped on a dime in front of me and spit up snow from her skis to the left of her. "Are you ready to go, First Class?" She pulled her scarf down just a bit. I could see that her nose was a red shade of brown.

"Hell nawl! You want me to go down that big-ass hill?"

"Yeah, it's so exhilarating and freeing. Whatever is on your heart right now, you will be able to release it while you're taking this dive. Come on, just trust me." She skied a bit forward and stopped.

"You do realize that this is my first time on skis, right? And that me trying to ski down this hill is basically suicide."

"Never. I showed you what to do for two hours. You're good. Just trust your instincts and this is going to be awesome. Let's go." She shot down the hill with a swipe of her sticks in the snow.

I slowly skirted to the edge of it like a little kid with a Pamper full of poop. I stopped and looked down at it. Jelissa was swerving from side to side like a professional. It must not have been that hard because she was making it look so easy. I closed my eyes and looked up to the heavens. "Jehovah, hold me down. If you take me, make sure you put me where my mother and sister is. I deserve whatever you got in mind. I know I've been a savage. Here goes nothing."

I pushed as hard as I could with the sticks in the snow and took off like a rocket. I went over the hill and picked up momentum right away. My stomach turned upside down. I was coasting, and a smile spread across my face.

Jelissa was skiing backwards and zigzagging. "There you go, TJ. That's what I'm talking about!" she hollered. She turned all the way around and began to ski normally.

I got to going faster and faster. The skis kept picking up more speed. Suddenly I got paranoid. I'd forgotten how to stop. I panicked. I dropped my right stick and dug the left one into the snow.

As soon as I did I jerked. The stick got stuck and made my left arm shudder. My right ski somehow hit a bump, and the next thing I knew I was hitting cartwheels all the way down the damn hill, eating a mouthful of snow. I hopped, I jumped, I spun sideways and wound up on my back with frosty smoke coming out of my nose and mouth. I couldn't do anything but lay there for a moment, broke up. Everything hurt.

Jelissa stopped by me and snow from her skis drenched my face. She knelt down in her hot pink snow suit. "Dang, TJ, are you okay?"

I closed my eyes. I was in so much pain. What the hell was I thinking? I frowned and sat up. "That's why black ma'fuckas don't ski right there." I stood up and ran over to one of the poles. I picked it up and threw it as far as I could. Then I tracked through the snow and grabbed the other one. When I got it, I ran through the snow and tossed it as far into the sky as I could.

While doing so, I wound up tripping and face planting in the snow. I rolled over and took my left ski off, stood up, and broke it over my knee. My sock was cold in the snow. I didn't care. Next came the right ski. I took it off and threw it down the hill. "Punk-ass skis!" I walked back to the cabin with my bare socks crunching the cold snow. I was pissed and ready to go back to Chicago.

Jelissa came up behind me, trying her best to hold in her laugh. "Aw, TJ, it's okay. At least you tried."

"Say, Jelissa, leave me alone right now. Straight up, I ain't in no mood for your ass." I stopped, balled up a snowball, and tried my best to rock her li'l slim ass but missed, then that pissed me off too.

***

Later that day, I sat in the room with my door locked, Facetiming with Tonya. She looked more depressed than I did.

"Damn, daddy, I miss you so much. Why didn't you take me with you?" She looked into the camera with her eyes glossy.

"I'm trying to figure some things out, li'l baby. I needed this mental break, but I'll be back home Monday. I miss you like a ma'fucka too though. Are you being strong for me?"

"No. I don't like this shit. I don't know how you expect me to go off to college when I can't be away from yo' ass for more than a day without my depression kicking in and taking me out the game. Damn, I love yo' crazy ass."

"I love you, too." We were quiet for a moment.

"Does this have anything to do with another bitch?" Tonya ran her fingers through her sandy brown hair. Her eyes were puffy, and I could tell that she had been crying.

"Yeah, and it's something that I gotta do too."

"That figures. Man, I wish these bitches would just leave you alone. I can handle you all to myself. I swear I can. You're my daddy, and I am crazy about you."

"I know you are, baby. Damn, I miss yo' li'l ass." I looked her over. "I need you for a minute, too."

"What you need, daddy? You already know I'm down."

I was thirsty as hell. "I need to see that pussy right quick so I can stay on the straight and narrow."

Tonya took a second to program what I was saying. When she got it, her eyes got big and she stood up. "Hold on, let me lock this door." She came back seconds later and sat on her bed. She scooted all the way back until her back was against her headboard. She moved her white T-shirt up, and flashed me her naked pussy lips. The hair was just starting to come back on them. "Can you see them?"

I was already doing my thing. Damn, I had never really realized how puffy she was down there. I imagined some of the things we had done when we were in New York and I was already on the verge of cumming. "Yeah, boo, I see 'em."

"Damn, daddy, let me see you, too. I'm feening for you just as bad."

I angled the phone so she could see my pipe while I pumped him. She started to moan. Her fingers went in between her sex lips. She pinched her clitoris and opened her pinkness wide for me to see. I shuddered and grew weak.

"Daddy, I love you. I love you so much. Fuck, I miss you!" she screamed into the computer.

I saw two of her fingers go into her, and that was enough for me. I grabbed the Kleenex and came all over it, imagining breaking her li'l ass up like I always did. "Fuck, li'l baby!" I clenched my teeth.

"Let me see it, daddy! Let me see that cum. Aw fuck!" She began to flop around on the bed, getting it. When she finished, she kept her fingers between her thick thighs. "Are you good now, daddy?"

I was straight. "Yeah, good looking, boo, I'ma hit you up in the morning. Daddy loves you."

"I love you too, daddy."

I went and jumped in the shower with everything coursing through my mind. I didn't think I was going to be able to stay in Colorado for the full time. While I appreciated Jelissa asking me to come out there with her, it was too boring for me. I missed Chicago, and I wanted to get back home to Tonya and my hood.

I finished showering in fifteen minutes and was on my way to telling Jelissa the decision I had made to leave, but when I got into the living room, she blew my mind.

Chapter 16

"Yo, what are you doing?" I noticed my notepads and my handwriting on them right away. Jelissa had a box of my manuscripts that I'd written while I was in St. Charles reformatory. I'd sent this box to Sodi just before I got out of prison.

She turned around and pulled her glasses off of her nose. She handed me her laptop. "Here, I want you to look this over. I've been taking my time to properly edit this book that you wrote while you were locked up, and I think I finally got it to where it is ready for the market. Have a look."

"How did you get all of this?"

"Before Sodi was able to get on her feet, she often stayed at my house from time to time because hers was too crowded with siblings. Long story short, this box of your manuscripts was the most important thing in the world to her. I don't know if she simply had the premonition that something tragic was about to happen to her, but she always said that if anything ever did to make sure that you didn't stop writing, and that these manuscripts were to be perfected. I've done more than that.

Not only have I perfected seven of your stories, but I've found you a company that is willing to give you a deal. They like your writing, and the sistah that is the COO of this company is thorough. We are in the same real estate circles and Black business women of America circles. We've talked greatly about you and she's willing to give you that shot."

My eyes were reading over the edited version of my story, *The Ski Mask Cartel*. I breezed through five quick chapters and began to nod my head. "Damn, this is good."

"I know, I couldn't put it down. I like this series, and the *King of New York* one. That one is flaming. I see this one here that you have labelled *Born Heartless* has my name in it. Are you going to finish it?"

"Yeah, I can't start somethin' and not finish it. I ain't never been able to do that. I got plenty of text from the other parts saved into my phone. Look." I went into my pocket and showed it to her.

She grabbed it and began reading over it. "Wow, you've gotten a whole lot better when it comes to your grammar. Shawn Walker says that before Sodi died, she reached out to her about giving you a contract, but you never followed up on it. She says that she liked you back then, but even more so now that she has a clearer understanding of who you are. I guess your name is ringing bells all the way back to Houston, Texas where she is from."

"I don't know anybody down south so I don't know how that could be so, but whatever. What kind of chips is she talking about?"

"They are willing to sign you on for fifteen thousand apiece for each book, and you'll get forty percent of your royalties for the rest of your life. At least, that's the understanding that I got, but I think that it's important for you to talk with her on your own. I'll punch her contact information into your phone. She is a powerful and amazing sistah, you'll see that first hand. But congratulations ahead of time." She smiled and handed the phone back to me.

I felt good because writing was a passion of mine. It was an escape. Whenever life became too much and I felt like I was too overwhelmed to press forward, I picked up my phone and I just wrote. Because of the fast life that I lived, I didn't think that I could ever run out of material. "Thank you for editing it like this. Now I can see what I am doing wrong."

"You're welcome. If I had to give you some advice, though, I would say that you need to factor in your female audience more. I mean, I get that this is how you really are when it comes to the money, drugs, and murder, but what you have to realize is that us women need more of a love story. We need subtle and real life moments. Touching parts of the book. We need to see character development, and times when the male character is vulnerable or maturing. Though this is the perfect depiction of what I know you to actually be, don't be afraid to tap into your emotions a little more."

I put the laptop down, and took a seat beside her. "How the fuck can I put my emotions into a book when I ain't even supposed to have them? My old man said that a man with emotions is nothing more than prey. He is at the bottom of the food chain and should be crushed."

"Your old man doesn't sound like he has any intelligence. God gave everybody emotions make and female, and He gave us His good book to show us how to control them. Having emotions doesn't make you weak, it makes you human. You said you cared about me, right?"

"Yeah, I do."

"Well, care is a form of emotions. And for the record, I care about you, too." She rested her hand on the side of my face.

"You sure about that?" I looked into her piercing brown eyes.

"Yeah, but I still wanna know what you see in me. Why doesn't my situation scare you?" She looked so fine by the fireplace fire. The scent of her perfume was heavy in the room.

"It's not that it doesn't scare me, but I find myself down to endure it because I really like you and I have from day one. I think that you are an incredibly beautiful and amazing woman. I like your style, your demeanor, and your intelligence. There is nothing sexier than an independent, intelligent, headstrong woman."

"You keep forgetting mother of two. One of those boys happens to be your nephew. That is the topic that we keep on skipping over." She stood up and stood in front of the fireplace.

I got up and stepped behind her, wrapping my arms around her waist. "I know who A'Jhani is, and I know that he comes from Deion and that there is going to be a whole lot of drama and backlash from that, but so what? Why can't we fight through that together? If we really wanna be together, we will find a way to conquer every obstacle that stands in our way, right?"

She nodded her head. "You trap all day. You got all of this money, women, and the world at your feet right now, TJ. I have two children by two different men and both of them are headaches. That is a lot of baggage, not to mention the fact that when I become involved with a man, I am very possessive. I want him to be mine and all mine. I don't have time for the games or nothing that comes along with it. I am confident yet selfish with my man. Ain't no such thing as you having two or three women while you are with me. Are you even sure that you could be in a relationship under those conditions?"

"Nope, I'm not sure. I have never seen a healthy relationship for as long as I have been alive. I don't know what it looks or feels like, but I am ready to see." I leaned my face into the crux of her neck. "What do you want?"

"I wanna run into a man that doesn't always know how to say the right things to get what he wants in the moment. I need an action man. A man that doesn't have the right words he only has the right actions. I need a man that will accept my circumstances and help me to thrive within them. I need a pure role model for my children. I need a consistent male figure that will guide them properly and without ceasing. I don't want his love for them to be wavered by our disagreements or misunderstandings. I don't want for my children to be used as a pawn, nor myself." She wiggled out of my embrace. "There aren't many real men left, TJ. Not for women like me." She stoked the fire with the poker. The wood crackled and popped loudly.

I stepped beside her, feeling the heat on my legs. "Jelissa, I don't know what all you have been through, but I'm sorry. I wish I could change your past, but all I can do is help to give you a better future, because that's what you deserve." I pulled her to me aggressively and pressed my forehead to hers. "I don't give a fuck what goes on. You can't stop me from caring about you. You remind me so much of my mother: broken, yet strong, physically beautiful, but your daily pains are as ugly as a beast."

I tilted her chin up so that she was looking into my eyes. "I wanna ride for you the best way that I know how. I know that I am not perfect, but I am willing to try as hard as I can for you until we figure it out and get things right. I know what I am up against and I am telling you that I won't fold. Take a gamble on me."

"TJ, when you are a mother of two, there is no room to take a gamble. You have to get it right each time. Everything that I do, whether good or bad, reflects on my children and my title as a mother. If I consider you, then I also have to consider how I will be able to explain it to my son that I am involved with his uncle when he gets older. How could I possibly tell my son that I married his uncle if we ever choose to go that route?"

"You will tell him just like you just said it. Why is the child allowed to be the determining factor for us? How can you find happiness if it always boils down to that?"

"I don't know. I guess that's why I invited you out here with me, to sort of convince myself that I am doing the right thing. That we have a chance at each other against all odds."

I pulled her to me again and kissed her lips, softly at first, and then with more vigor. "Jelissa, I need you. I need you because the world is telling me that I am not supposed to have you. Whenever anybody denies me something, I go for it with everything that I have. I don't give up, I refuse to."

"Yeah, but I don't want to be some joystick, or for you to treat my real life situation like a video game. I don't wanna be your pawn in this sibling rivalry that you have with your brother Deion. If you really care about me, and if you really want to be with me, then you will fight beside me and never leave, even when things get rough and out of place. The man that I seek will never abandon me. He will never forsake me. He is God-fearing and devoted to me, his Eve. How can you be sure that this is you?"

I was rubbing her soft cheeks with the backs of my fingers. Our eyes were locked. I could feel her breathing on my neck, the scent of her perfume coupled with that of the fireplace. "Because I am willing to fight for you. I need you, and I wanna be that every man. I need that unconditional love that I know you can render to me. I've never had it, and I crave it." I kissed her lips softly. "Can you please give me a chance? Please. Show me how to love. I am willing to drop my ego so that I can learn. I am willing to sacrifice what I am familiar with in order to step into the unknown of what I didn't know existed. I want you. Only you, wholeheartedly. Now can you give me a chance?" I kissed her again.

"I don't know. I'm so torn right now. I don't want to be a fad that you are experiencing. I want – no, I need - for your feelings to be real and not false. I don't want them to fade. A woman can only take so much heartache before she is scorned.

I have never been closer to that point than I am right now. So if you needed me to give you an answer about us, right now, my answer is no."

My heart sank. I released her and stepped back. "Really?"

She nodded. "Yeah, I just don't see how it could work out. We are headed into two different directions, and our struggles aren't similar in the least bit. I am not an asset to you, but a pull me down, and likewise, you are to me also. I'm sorry, TJ, I wish things were different." She walked away from me with tears in her eyes.

I stood there for a long time, lost and not knowing what to say or do. Instead of staying there and constantly going back and forth with Jelissa, I packed my things and jumped on the first first-class flight back to Chicago. I didn't even let her know that I was leaving.

***

Tonya was waiting at the airport for me when I got off of the plane. She ran and jumped into my arms. I turned her around and around, holding her with a big smile on my face. When I set her down, she wrapped her arms around my neck and kissed my lips passionately. We tongued each other down for ten straight minutes. I was ready to fuck her right there in the airport in front of everybody before we finally broke apart.

She took a step back and wiped her mouth. "Daddy, we found where Deion lay his head at. Juelz was going to send a few of your hittas to finish him, but I figured you'd want to have that privilege, so I stopped him. But you gotta get back to the hood fast. Things are about to get real super fast." She hugged me tightly again. "Damn, I'm so glad that you're back!"

"It feels good to be home, li'l baby, trust and believe when I tell you that it does."

Chapter 17

Juelz's eyelids closed slowly. He leaned against the passenger's door and began to scratch his inner forearm. "Man, shorty, I'm fucked up right now. I should have never tried that dog food from south of the border." He scratched his arm some more until his nails filled up with blood.

I was disgusted. I couldn't believe what I was looking at. "Bruh, what, you shooting that shit now or somethin'?" I frowned at him from the driver's seat of my Navigator. He didn't smell so good and he could barely keep his eyes open. This wasn't the Juelz that I was accustomed to being around.

"Say, man, don't you get on my case too. I already got my daughter's mother sweating me about this bullshit. I was down for almost a year and you didn't even know. You know why you didn't know?" He nodded off with his lips pursed together.

I sat there mugging him. "Why, nigga? Damn!"

His eyelids opened. "Because I got this shit under control." He let his seat back and patted his shirt pocket. He pulled out a cigarette.

I snatched it from his hand. "You got me fucked up. You smoke squares and you shooting dope. Shorty, you done fell all the way off."

"Never that, Jo, never that right there." He opened his eyes and sat back up. His lips smacked together. He looked around as if he was missing something. "Where my shit go?"

I broke the cigarette and threw that nasty-ass shit out of the window. "Fuck that square! What's up with Deion? Where dis nigga laying his head at?"

"That's how you do me?" He leaned into the passenger's window and rested his face on the glass. "Just treat me like a chump. But that's awright because when Jordan was on the

Bulls, the city was lit." He broke into laughter and slapped his thigh.

"What, nigga? What are you talking about?" I pushed his ass.

He covered his head and then opened his eyes as big as he could get them. "Nawl, on some real shit, though, that nigga stay out in Harvey, a few blocks over from Riverdale. He got a li'l snow bunny out there that's supposed to be Arab or somethin'. He calls her Li'l Moon. I think her real name is Serena. She used to go to school with us back in the day before she moved back home to Jordan. She was a real stuck-up and religious chick back then. I don't know how he knocked her seeing as he does more dope than I do. Which ain't much, so don't get it twisted." He closed his eyes again and scratched the same spot that he'd been scratching all night.

"Who all stays there with him? Is it a little boy? You know, about a year old?" I was worried about Jelissa's kid being hit in the crossfire if shit was to go down, which I was a hundred percent sure that it was.

"Nigga, I don't know if he got kids in there or not. I know his Arab bitch just had a shorty. I don't know if he's the father or what, but I assume so." He sat up and looked around outside of the truck.

It was pitch dark outside. We were in the parking lot of my project buildings right off of Howard Street. All of the street lamps and cameras had been busted out. My troops roamed the hood with flashlights and those little black helmets with the flashlights on top of them. I knew my hood inside and out and so did the killas that were working directly under me. I didn't care if anybody else could navigate my slums as long as we could.

"Say, dawg, we need to ice that nigga though. I got wind that he is supposed to be trying to move out north with his crew and some mo' niggas he done formed an alliance with. I think that you may be a serious target, and if that is the case, then it is only a matter of time before you are feeling those hot ones. I heard this fool found a way to integrate religion into his gang shit. That's dangerous."

"Right, that is. So fuck it, let's move on his goofy ass tonight. What's stopping us?" I was ready to go. I grabbed the Tech .9 from under my seat and set that heavy bitch on my lap. I could already imagine gunning Deion's ass down and I know I should have been feeling some type of way because he was my half-brother, but all I felt was pure adrenaline coursing through me. Jelissa's kid came across my mind, but I would handle that situation when I approached it.

Juelz scratched his neck and groaned. "Shorty, you already know it's whatever wit' me. What, you wanna roll through that bitch right now on some bloody shit? What it is?" He talked with his eyes closed.

To answer his question, I put the truck in drive and pulled off. I had Tee Grizzley playing in the background. His music most fit my personality. "Yo, when we get over there, shorty, I don't give a fuck what you do, but you make sure that I am the one to punch his lights out. Don't nobody kill Deion but me. That's my birthright, you got that?"

He snickered. "You should have whacked his ass a long time ago. If you had, we wouldn't be going through all of this shit the way that we are. Now this nigga done got all powerful and shit. We don't know what the retaliation is going to be like. But fuck it, I'm born heartless, nigga."

"Nawl, *we* were *born* heartless, get that right," I corrected him and kept rolling.

"Whatever happened with that Jelissa bitch you were supposed to go skiing wit'? Did you know that she was supposed to have had a baby by Deion and that fuck nigga Reggie that Punkin claiming her cousin?"

I slammed on the brakes and the truck slid down the street and stopped. "What the fuck you just say?"

Now Juelz was alert and looking around on some paranoid type shit. "Shorty, roll off, all dese ma'fuckin' Cobras be over here, and them niggas got cannons. I ain't tryna get aired out. Fuck wrong wit' you?" he snapped.

I stepped back on the gas just as about twelve Latinos stepped into the middle of the street with guns in their hands. A tall skinny one, heavily tatted, threw his arms up. More started to come out of the gangways of the houses on the block. Then they began to block the street behind us.

"Shit, you see what you done did?" Juelz cocked his Draco. He rolled down the window and stuck out his head. "Yo, we ain't mean no disrespect. Our brakes fuckin' up, if y'all will let us pass on this indiscretion."

The Latinos didn't play in Chicago. They would shoot yo' ass dead, especially if you were caught out of bounds in their hood the way that we were. I wasn't about to let their asses kill me. If they didn't give Juelz permission soon, I was about to let that Tech scream like a white girl in a scary movie.

The tall Latino in the front stepped to the side and waved for us to pass. A sigh of relief came over me. I stepped on the accelerator and rolled past them with all of them mugging us as if they wanted to kill us. Juelz sat back down and checked behind him as we got the corner of their hood. I made a right and we were in the clear.

"Now, what were you saying?"

"First of all, don't slam on yo' brakes no more. You almost got us killed, damn." He checked over his shoulder again and then sat back in his seat. He took the pink Sprite that was laced with codeine from the center console and turned it up. While twisting the cap back on, he began to talk. "It turns out that Punkin's so-called cousin is the same nigga that got a baby by Jelissa. I guess their son's name is Ray John or some shit like that."

"Rae'Jon; but go 'head."

"That's what I said, nigga, damn." He set his bottle back into the console. "Anyway, they all went to Verona High School together. Reggie is originally from Des Moines, Iowa. He spent a few years in Chicago though, where he went to high school, and anyway, he was supposed to have been Jelissa's first. Got her pregnant the first time he hit, then broke camp.

He a real deadbeat-ass nigga and do the bare minimum for the kid and all of that. Also, that nigga ain't no kin to Punkin either. When you was locked up, he was fucking her. Her own sister Shanay told me this and she doesn't front when it comes to that real life shit. She said that Punkin ain't never stopped fuckin' dude and that it's a good chance that li'l dawg ain't even yo' son, that he's his, or…and wait for this." He smiled. "Or he might be Deion's."

"Deion's?" I almost slammed on the brakes again, but refrained.

"Yeah, nigga, Deion's. Deion been fuckin' her since high school. Shanay says the last time they were together was like two days ago. That bitch is dirty. So is Deion, and so is Reggie. I think Jelissa just got dealt a bad hand because I couldn't pull up no dirt on her. Everybody says she is a homebody that sticks to investing in the community and running her businesses. I still can't see how she got involved with Deion, but then again, that nigga running around all of the bitches."

"I can't believe that my son might be his. That shit ain't right. And why wouldn't Jelissa keep shit one hunnit wit' me?

Why wouldn't she tell me that Rae'Jon's father was Reggie's bitch ass? Fuck!" I felt so betrayed that I felt like killing somethin'.

"As hard as I know those pills are to swallow, that ain't it." He lowered his head and shook it. "I found out through some intensive digging that Punkin paid Reggie to rob and kill Sodi. That shit was a set-up. Sodi trusted Punkin. They were best friends. That's why there wasn't any forced entry. That night, both Reggie and Punkin came to Sodi's house while we were in Jamaica and Punkin watched her nigga kill yo' first love. She had him kill her because she wanted you all to herself. That bitch is evil and conniving."

My head was spinning. I couldn't think straight. I felt like I was getting ready to pass out. There were so many facts coming at me that I didn't think my brain could process them all at one time. "Yo, how do you know all of this?"

"When that shit happened to you with the skillet, I put the hunters out to find that fool Reggie, and I did a lot of digging. That's how I came up with all of these facts, plus you wouldn't believe how many of the hoes that used to go to school with us are hopped up on pills and heroin. I got a lot of loyal customers from our school, including a lot of the teachers."

I nodded my head. "That's why it's so hard to trust anybody out here. It doesn't make sense to. Ma'fuckas ain't loyal. Especially these punk-ass bitches. Yo, I swear to Jehovah, if I find out that that baby ain't mine, I'm snuffing shorty. She gotta go. I already fell in love with him. I see so much of myself in my seed."

"I know, homie, but everything happens for a reason. Punkin is shiesty and very selfish. Can you imagine what it would be like to have her as a baby mother? She'll probably keep a nigga in and out of the bing. That's if she doesn't set you up to be killed. You see how much she really cares about you already. She hit yo' ass over the head with a pan for that fool Reggie. That says a lot. Only time a female gon' shed yo' blood is if she doesn't give two fucks about you. Clearly she doesn't. You may have caught a blessing. Have you ever thought about it like that?"

"Man, I ain't had time to digest none of this shit. I'm sick as a bitch. These are too many twists for me. I don't know who to go at first." I felt like I was about to throw up. That sick feeling resonated all over me.

"We go at Deion first. That's where we are headed to. That's the nigga that's gon' get clapped tonight. It's as simple as that." Juelz adjusted his Draco on his lap. "I been wanting to kill that shiesty-ass nigga. He murdered a lot of my li'l homies and would have murdered me twice when you were locked up, but a few of my youngin's took those slugs. I never told you that either, but it's the truth."

"Dawg, if you tell me one more secret that you kept from me, we gon' have a serious-ass problem. Fuck. Let's just roll in silence."

"Yeah, a'ight, nigga, let's do that then."

We rolled for the next thirty minutes in absolute silence. It was so quiet in the truck that all you could hear was the sounds of the tires of the Navigator rolling over the tore-up-ass streets of Chicago. The roads were so bad that I constantly worried about my wheels and suspension coming out of alignment. It was ridiculous.

When we finally pulled into Harvey, Juelz sat up and became alert. He placed his hand around the Draco. "Yo, take this block right here and ride this ma'fucka to the end of the street and make a right. You gon' see a bunch of brick houses. His shit got a metal gate around it."

I followed his directives until I came to the corner of Deion's block. I stopped at the stop sign and noticed that there were four police cars parked in front of his house and two across the street from it. Looking down the street, there was a team of police officers in task force gear creeping down the street. They stopped at his house and pulled open the gate. Then they were rushing into his yard and up the stairs in raid mode.

"We ain't finna get at that nigga tonight." I threw the truck in reverse and pulled off of his strip. I made a backwards U-turn and headed back toward the inner city of Chicago.

"Damn, bruh, what you think them people on wit' him?" Juelz kept checking the rearview mirror and over his shoulder.

"I don't know, but whatever he did, I hope he comes from under that jam. I can only wait so much longer before I get the chance to smoke his ass." I had never felt more vengeful than I did right then. "Bruh, tonight ma'fuckas finna give me some answers or I'm about to tear this city apart. That's on my mother."

"You already know I'm riding wit' you until the wheels fall off. Let's get to it."

"Nawl, I need to get these answers on my own. Where do you want me to drop you off at? I can tell you need to get some sleep anyway."

Juelz laughed. "Aw, you know shit is about to get real emotional and you don't want me to be around when you go there, huh? That's cool; I can dig that. Just drop me back off over in the Holy City. I gotta touch bases with a few of the fellas anyway.

Whenever you feel like you want me to come and roll out with you, all you gotta do is give me a call and I'll be there. Until then, I got some shit I gotta handle on my own." He ran his hand over his face and frowned. "Yeah, I gotta take care of my own bidness."

I wanted to ask him what that business pertained to, but I decided against that. I didn't care at that moment. I'd heard that Jelissa had flown back to Chicago already and I needed to get up with her. I felt that if Juelz was with me that she wouldn't be open with me. She was already fuming because of how I'd left her back in Colorado.

So I drove Juelz to the Holy City and let him out. We shook up in silence, and I headed off into the night with a laser focus of getting all of the answers that I needed for my own psyche.

Chapter 18

I didn't even give Jelissa time to ask me to come into her home. As soon as she opened the door, I rushed inside and stood mugging her. "When was you gon' tell me that Punkin's cousin was your baby daddy?"

"What?" She closed the front door.

"Don't what me, Jelissa, that bitch-ass nigga Reggie. That's your oldest son's father, right?"

"Yeah, but I didn't know that he and her were supposed to be cousins. She used to mess with him back when we were all going to school. It's impossible for them to be family. Wait a minute, what's going on here?"

I was steaming because she was so calm. I couldn't tell if she was lying or telling the truth. "Look, man, I just found out that the kid I got with Punkin might not be mine. He could belong to this Reggie nigga, or even Deion. My head is a little fucked up right now and I need some answers. Why didn't you tell me that Deion was fuckin' Punkin'?"

"Because that is not my business and I have never been in the bedroom while they were doing anything. I don't spread lies about people. I am a grown woman. Why are you bringing all of this to me and not them? This doesn't make any sense."

She was right. Why was I coming at her instead of trying to go directly to the source, which was Punkin and Deion? "I don't know. I guess I figured I'd work from the bottom up."

"And I'm the bottom? Is that why you didn't have the decency to tell me that you were leaving Colorado? Is that why you had me make you breakfast in bed but when I went to your room, all I found was a short note saying that you were gone?" She scoffed. "I don't even know why I opened the door for you, TJ, it's three in the morning."

I was pacing back and forth. "My son...you saw him, right?"

"Excuse me?" She stepped forward and raised her left eyebrow.

"Junior. You've seen pictures of him. Does he look like your youngest son to you? Could he be Deion's baby?"

She picked her phone up from the table and began to scroll through it. When she was done, she handed me the phone. "I've already been where you are right now. Not emotionally, but just wondering. I think there is a strong possibility that Junior is Deion's son."

I looked down the long row of pictures. She had them set up so that it had A'Jhani on the left side and beside him was Junior. They looked identical. It was so scary that I felt a chill go down my spine. I had been betrayed. I handed her phone back to her. "Why didn't you tell me this?"

"It's not my place to. This isn't my business. But what I can say is that I was sure that you knew, and I thought the whole reason that you pursued me was because you wanted to get back at Deion for knocking her up. I mean, if he did it. I didn't for one second think that you had any genuine feelings toward me, but now that I see you were oblivious to all of this, TJ, I am so sorry. I never gave you a chance." She stepped toward me and took a hold of my wrists.

I yanked them away from her. "Yo, is Reggie your baby daddy?"

She nodded. "He is Rae'Jon's father, but he and I have only been physical three times. The first time we laid down, I got pregnant. We were in high school. After Rae'Jon was born, we tried to make it work for a few months or so. We slept together twice, and there was no flame. He walked out and hasn't done anything for my son ever since then. We have no relationship. He is a deadbeat, as much as it pains me to say that."

"So why didn't you tell me who he was to you when I told you about them pretty much jumping me and shit?"

"You never said a name. All you kept saying was that it was Punkin and her cousin, and I never pried. However, I apologize. I apologize for holding secrets from you, and for not being as transparent as I should have been. You deserved more than that. Please forgive me. I am seeing you through new eyes now that I am sure you didn't ever have a hidden agenda." She hugged my body tightly.

I was so mad and so furious that I wanted to snap out. I wanted to lose my mind and go ballistic, but I had to chill and calm myself. Before I could even control what I was doing, I was holding her. "Damn, Jelissa, my mind is fucked up right now. All I can think about is killing a ma'fucka. Punkin, Reggie, Deion, all of them. I can't even think straight." I began to shake.

She stepped back and rested her hands on my chest. "TJ, in the spirit of being transparent, I need to let you know how much I like you. Like I said before, I thought that you had something up your sleeve and that you were trying to use me as some sort of pawn, but even then, I couldn't help but to feel a way for you.

I think that you are a very handsome, strong, warm-hearted, and different kind of man. All I do is think about you, and even though you pissed me clean off when you left me looking stupid over in Colorado, at least you weren't a total dick about it, and you actually paid for my ticket to be upgraded to first class even though I never asked you for that. That was kind of cool. But I say that to say that I truly like you, and I'm not afraid for us to step into that forbidden realm of things.

If you truly feel that you can be that man that I need you to be against all of these odds, then I am sure that I can ride by your side no matter what. I know that you have a lot of things that you need to figure out, but you need to know that I am not one of them. I am yours if you want me." She stepped on her pedicured toes and kissed me on the lips, soft at first, and then with more passion. Her arms wrapped around my neck.

I allowed her to kiss me at first without me so much as making a move. Then suddenly I felt her tongue swipe my lips. They opened and we began to make out like horny teenagers on prom night. I picked her up. She wrapped her ankles around me. We continued to kiss and moan into each other's mouths. I was getting heated. While murder was still going through my mind, now I began to think about sexing her body.

I carried her through the house and sat her on the edge of her kitchen table. I stripped right in front of her and leaned her all the way back, pulling her short blue nightgown up to her hips. Her sex lips were molded to the fabric of her panties. My face entered into the apex of her thighs. I kissed her pussy through the material.

"I'm lost right now, Jelissa."

More kissing. I pulled the cloth to the side and exposed her naked sex. The lips were dark brown and already moist with her dew. My tongue attacked up and down her slit. I peeled the lips wide open until her pink was exposed. She was oozing already. I licked into her crease and dipped my tongue in and out of her at full speed while my nose bumped her clitoris on purpose. She leaked all over it. When I locked on to her vagina's nipple with my lips, she arched her back and moaned loudly.

"Unnnn! TJ! Are you sure you wanna do this right now?" She sucked her bottom lip.

I looked up and pulled her shoulder straps off of her shoulder one at a time until it was around her waist. Her titties popped out. They were small with hard nipples, perfect for me. I pulled her back to the edge of the table and began to eat her as if I was starving. My focus was on her erect clitoris.

"Uh! Uhhhh! Shoot! TJ! You gon' make me… You gon' make me…!" She bucked into my face, pushing it further into her pussy with her left hand while she rotated her hips in a circular motion.

I slurped and licked. Her juices ran down my neck all the way to my stomach. She squirmed all over the table. Then she screamed and stuffed my face into her gap while she wrapped her ankles around my shoulders. I couldn't breathe, but at the same time, I didn't care. Her pleasure was important.

She started to shake. "Shoot! Shoot! Aww shit!" She came, screaming and trembling.

I kept licking, sucking, and swallowing. "Cum, Jelissa!" I growled.

"Awwwwww!" She pushed me away and scooted back on the table.

I pulled her li'l ass back to me and made her thighs go around my waist. I lined myself up and slipped deep into her tight pussy. "Mmm!" I stayed planted as deep as I could for a second. Then I pulled all the way back and began to stroke her like a savage.

Clap! Clap! Clap! Clap!

"Unnn! Unnn! Unnn! Shit!" She threw her head back and dug her nails into my shoulder blades. She scooted forward harder and faster every time I pumped forward. "Unh! Unh! Unh! Do dat! Do dat, TJ!" She opened her mouth wide. Her breasts jiggled up and down on her small frame while she took the pipe deep.

I growled and licked her neck. "Dis my shit now! Mmm! Mmm! Mmm! Dis mine, Jelissa! I gotta have you!" I held her more firmly and began to go haywire on that pussy, taking out my anger and frustrations. It was so good. "Tell me it's mine!" I slammed it harder. Pulled her to me more.

"It's yours, TJ! Damn! It's yours!"

I sucked on her neck and bit into it with my teeth, ramming her stroke for stroke. She shivered and came again. I pulled out and bent her li'l ass over the table, took a hold of her hips, and rocked her from the back, long stroking her inch by inch.

While fuckin', I couldn't help but to rub all over her and slap that ass. She was thick. It jiggled a lot and encouraged me to go harder. Her juices ran down my inner thighs, and my finger slipped into her back door. I shivered. I bit into the back of her neck and came back to back, groaning. "Uhhhhh fuck! Uhhh, Jelissa! Fuck, baby!"

She smashed her pussy back into my lap over and over again roughly. She tensed up and screamed again. "Shit! Shit! Shit!" She came and fell chest first into the table.

I remained planted deep within her. We wound up on the kitchen floor lying on our sides. I pulled her back to me and kissed all over her neck. "You gon' be my fuck the world symbol. I'm choosing you. Fuck everybody, Jelissa."

"What do you mean, TJ?" She snuggled more into me.

"Everybody gon' say I'm bogus for cuffing you and building a life with you because you are Deion's baby mother, but fuck them. You are my forbidden slice of heaven. You are how I'm gon' to say fuck everybody."

Jelissa was quiet. "That's not what I want. All I need is for you to love me and treat me like your Queen. I promise to be the best woman for you that I can be if you will promise to be the best man for me."

I didn't know what to say to that. I had so much growing up to do. All I knew was that I really cared about her. She made me feel different in a good way, and she reminded me so much of my mother that it was scary. Second to that, I felt like a piece of Sodi was living inside of her. I needed Jelissa. I craved her. I didn't give a fuck about the naysayers. I was going to make her mine.

"Jelissa, can you teach me how to love? Can you be patient with me? Can you give me a chance to get better? Please, baby."

She rolled all the way around until we were facing each other. "I will." Her hand rested on my face. "I got you, TJ, and I ain't gon' never give up on you. That's my right hand to our Father in heaven. Do you got me?"

"Until my last breath. But I need you to accept me even after I do what I'm going to do to Reggie n'em."

Her fingers traced my lips. "What are you going to do, baby?"

"I don't want you to have the knowledge, but let's just say that's when it's all said and done, your boys will only have me as a father, and ain't shit you can do to stop me. I got them. I promise for the rest of my life."

"But why? Why would you do all of this? There has to be another way. Maybe we should pray about it. Please."

I shook my head. "Afterwards, because I'ma need that forgiveness. But I got this." I kissed her lips, and we laid in silence forehead to forehead for the rest of the night. My mind was already made up when the sun made its presence in the sky the next day. It was time to get on business.

T.J. Edwards

Chapter 19

Tonya slid into the passenger's seat and adjusted the .380 pistol on her hip. "Daddy, I still don't know why this gotta be my last move with you. I can go to school and still do what I gotta do out here. You're trying to turn me into a straight square and I don't like it." She sat back and crossed her arms in front of her with her bottom lip poked out.

She looked adorable to me. "Li'l baby, I already told yo' li'l ass that all I want you to focus on is school. The hood is about to change in a dramatic way. I ain't even about to be down here. I'm taking most of the bread I got put up and starting a publishing company. I'ma try to turn over a new leaf. This shit out here ain't what's good no more."

"A publishing company? Why?" She looked as if she had bitten into a rotten apple.

"Because I love to write, and I wanna have somethin' to offer my kids whenever I have them. This dope boy shit ain't gon' last forever. Sooner or later a ma'fucka gotta get ahead of the curve."

"Yeah, well, I guess. I don't know where all of this stuff is coming from all of a sudden, but it is what it is. You know I will follow you to the moon and back." She sighed. "My mother loves you for handling all of her bills for the year. She was even happier when she saw that I got a full ride to Clark University.

She said that you are one of the few good men that are left in the world and that I should better myself, get baptized, and marry you. I agreed with her." She looked out the passenger's window. "Are you really about to be with that Jelissa broad? I mean, do you even know her, and what does she have on me? I wanna kill her." Her eyes became watery.

I nodded my head. "Yeah, baby. I gotta try. That doesn't mean that I'm gon' forget about you. Daddy will never forget about his li'l girl. Dat shit'll never happen. I promise. Come here."

"Nope, I ain't feeling you right now, TJ. I thought you loved me. If you do, then how could you ever choose another female over me? I am supposed to be your world." She set her gun on her lap and started to break down crying into her hands. "You never choose me, ever."

I slid across the console of the Navigator and got into the seat with her. She sat on my lap and cried into my neck. "I love you, li'l boo. You're my baby. It's just not meant for us to be together like that. You deserve better. That's why I'm sending you to college, so you can be better and achieve all that you were meant to achieve. That doesn't mean that I'm kicking you to the curb though."

"Well, that's what it feels like. I love you with all of my heart! You're all I have. Don't nobody love me like you do. I can't believe you're going to crush me like this!" she screamed. "I'm not enough! You take pity on me. I hate you! I hate me, daddy!" She opened the passenger's door. I grabbed her. She yanked away from me. "Get off of me!" She slammed the door in my face. "I can't take the pain that you are putting me through. It's too much. I hate this! I - ."

Vroooooom! Bam!

A platinum Bentley truck slammed into Tonya at full speed, knocking her up into the air fifty feet before she came down awkwardly on her back. She rolled over, and remained still. Time seemed like it stood still. I was frozen in place. Before I could gather enough strength, the window to the tinted window of the Bentley truck rolled down. Deion stuck his head out of it. Half of his face was covered by a red rag. "Bitch-ass nigga, I heard you was looking for me." The

Bentley doors popped open and his shooters rushed out of them with assault rifles in their hands.

Boom! Boom! Boom! Boom!

The windows of my truck exploded. I ducked down and threw the truck in drive, stepping on the gas. I peeled away from the curb in the nick of time. More bullets rang out and shattered my back window. I stayed ducked down. Bullets shot through the passenger's seat right where Tonya had been sitting. I worried about her. I prayed to God she was okay. I felt sick.

I hit the corner and made a right just as Juelz and his troops sped toward Deion and his crew. I heard a series of gunfire and tires burning rubber. That nigga had caught me slipping and I felt like a gotdamn fool.

***

Tonya was laid up in the hospital for a week in critical condition. I visited her every single day without fail. I kissed her forehead and told her that I loved her with all of my heart. I relieved her mother of the burden of paying her hospital bills. I took care of all of that.

While she was in the hospital, me and my soldiers tore Chicago up looking for Deion. There was no more playing and no more mercy coming from me. I made sure that Jelissa took her sons and disappeared to New Jersey while I went on a rampage. She assured me that she would stay away from the action and that she would be waiting for me whenever I finished doing what I needed to do in the slums.

After the second week, Tonya had been moved out of the intensive care unit and into a normal room in the hospital, where she was still on a few machines. She awoke the third day of the second week and brightened up when she found me sitting on the side of her bed. I jumped up and began to kiss all over her face and forehead. She kept smiling.

"I'm okay, daddy, you can calm down." Her voice was thick with dryness.

I kissed her li'l white lips and grabbed her juice box. "Here, li'l baby, drink from this."

She did. "How long have I been here?"

"Don't matter, you're woke now. I knew yo' li'l ass was a fighter like me."

"Just like my daddy." She smiled. "My hips hurt."

"You broke them when you were hit by the truck. They hooked you up though, you're going to be okay." I kissed her forehead again.

"Do I still gotta go to college away from you? Please say no."

I laughed. "Hell yeah, you do. I want what's best for you. They say you'll be able to leave here in a few days, and then you'll need a li'l rehab. You should be walking by winter."

She nodded. "Thank you, daddy. I mean, for everything. You really are the best. I'm sorry for being so stupid. I just love you so much."

I held her face and kissed her lips. "I know, boo, that's why I will always have your back, because I love you, too. We gon' get through this shit together, I promise."

"Will you always make time for me, even when you are with her?"

I nodded. "Always. I got you."

"Then that is all that matters. I can respect your happiness and play my role. Can you just baby me for a few days? And then I'll be good. At least until I get out of the hospital? That's all I ask."

"Sure, baby, let me get up here with you so I can hold you. It's all good. We gon' make this time all about you."

She smiled. "I promise that after I leave this hospital that I will be able to let you live your life and I will work on mastering my own. Maybe there is something else out there that is better than the slums. I know I have to at least try to find it. Life is too precious."

"I agree, boo, but for now, just let daddy hold you." And I did for the next two days straight until she was strong enough to leave that hospital.

***

Three days later, Juelz hit me up and told me to meet him at the Rockwell Projects on the west side of Chicago. That he had a present for me. I damn near broke every speed limit in the city to get to him.

When I got there, his troops led me to the roof of the building. It was bright and sunny outside, so up on that roof was scorching hot. There were about fifty dudes up there dressed in black shorts and red shirts with bandannas around their faces.

I parted the crowd and found Juelz standing in the middle of them in front of a duct taped and gagged Reggie. Reggie's face was mangled and bloodied. Behind Juelz were two shirtless muscle-bound dark-skinned dudes holding red-nosed pit bulls. Juelz handed me a paper. I looked it over and saw that it was a DNA test for Junior. It read that Deion was ninety nine point nine percent possible to be the father. My heart sunk.

"Yeah, bruh, we couldn't find Deion's bitch ass, and Punkin fled to South Carolina, but we found this nigga dope dating one of the seventeen-year-old heroin junkies. What you wanna do wit' him?" Juelz asked, kneeling down into Reggie's face.

I was still sick over the piece of paper I held in my hand. I wanted to know how he'd gotten a hold of the information so quickly. I wanted to know why Punkin would play me. What had I ever done to her? I didn't have the physical strength to finish Reggie's bitch ass. "Yo, Juelz, dem dogs bite?"

Juelz laughed and stood up. "You muthafuckin' right they do. They only eat raw meat. What are you saying?"

I balled the paperwork upon my hand. "Shred this chump."

Juelz nodded at his homeboys. They stepped forward with their dogs barking and trying to break the leash. Juelz slapped Reggie's face. He took a knife and cut his cheeks up until flaps of skin were hanging. Reggie hollered and blood dripped out of his wounds. He struggled to break free. Juelz made the crowd stand back, and then the pit bulls were released. They attacked Reggie viciously, biting and ripping his face and neck apart. He hollered for ten minutes until he couldn't talk because his neck was gushing so much blood and plasma.

I stood back and watched. I felt nothing. No relief. No happiness. No sadness. Nothing. I walked away from the scene before it was all said and done. I was lost.

***

Lacey, Tonya's best friend, called my phone early one Sunday morning whispering. "TJ, I need for you to come to the Village right now. I got Deion's ass in here laid out. We been fuckin' and drinking all night. He is fucked up. I know what he did to my best friend and his bitch ass gotta pay. Please hurry up," she whispered.

When I got there twenty minutes later, Deion was still in the bed laid out butt ass naked. There was a packet of heroin on the dresser and a syringe as well. It smelled rank inside the room. But I didn't have no time to pinch my nose. I put my

.45 on safety and turned that bitch around, holding the barrel. I raised it far over my head and brought it down at full speed into the side of Deion's face. The first hit split him wide open. He hollered and bucked his eyes wide. I hit his bitch ass again.

"Wake yo' punk ass up!" I hollered.

He tried to get up, but I was all over him beating him over and over with the gun. His skull opened. Blood rushed out. He swung and hit me in the jaw. It didn't faze me. I kept beating him over and over with the vision of my mother coming into my mind. Then I saw Marie. I really fucked him up. When Tonya came into my psyche, he was lying on the floor lifeless with his mouth wide open. I constantly beat him over and over until Juelz pulled me off of him.

"Bruh! Bruh! Calm down, that nigga gone. Look at him." He pointed.

Deion looked like a smashed pumpkin. There was blood all over the room. The chrome gun was now red. My clothes were drenched and I was breathing hard as hell.

"I'ma have the homies chop him up and burn his ass. Then we gon' tackle this room. Go on and get out of here. I got this." He kicked Deion in the face hard.

"Awright, bruh." I staggered out of the room feeling elated. I had to get out of Chicago. There wasn't anything left for me here.

***

A few months later, I saw Tonya off to college. It was a proud moment for me, even though she didn't want to leave me. It was in her best interest because now she is a child psychologist and happily married with two children. Me and her stay in contact through social media, but that's it. I know that I am her weakness and I don't want her to jeopardize everything that she has worked so hard for, so I stay away out of love for her.

Punkin and I never spoke again. She sent me a Facebook message apologizing for lying to me about junior, though he still has my name. I never responded and I never plan on speaking to her ass ever again. I know my temper, and it's in her best interest that we stay in lost touch.

Juelz turned his dirty money clean by opening three strip clubs in Atlanta. He also started a record label and plugged in with Quality Control. He's seeing M's right now, and I applaud that switch up of the game. We are close and always will be.

Me and Jelissa are happily married and going strong. We hit the book game hard, drop series full of heat back to back, and count our blessings on a daily basis. While it has been hard to stay out of those streets, I find myself escaping through the pages of the books I write just to relive that madness. I know a lot of people would have gone crazy experiencing and doing most of the things that I have. How could a man knock off his own siblings and go about his life like it's the most natural thing in all of the world? Shit, I don't even know. I guess all I can say is that I was born heartless, and revenge is a dish best served cold. My mother and my sister deserved retribution. I made ma'fuckas pay for them. I regret nothing.

The End

Submission Guideline

Submit the first three chapters of your completed manuscript to ldpsubmissions@gmail.com, subject line: Your book's title. The manuscript must be in a .doc file and sent as an attachment. Document should be in Times New Roman, double spaced and in size 12 font. Also, provide your synopsis and full contact information. If sending multiple submissions, they must each be in a separate email.

Have a story but no way to send it electronically? You can still submit to LDP/Ca$h Presents. Send in the first three chapters, written or typed, of your completed manuscript to:

LDP: Submissions Dept
Po Box 944
Stockbridge, Ga 30281

DO NOT send original manuscript. Must be a duplicate.

Provide your synopsis and a cover letter containing your full contact information.

Thanks for considering LDP and Ca$h Presents.

T.J. Edwards

BOW DOWN TO MY GANGSTA

By **Ca$h**

TORN BETWEEN TWO

By **Coffee**

THE STREETS STAINED MY SOUL **II**

By **Marcellus Allen**

BLOOD OF A BOSS **VI**

SHADOWS OF THE GAME II

By **Askari**

LOYAL TO THE GAME **IV**

By **T.J. & Jelissa**

A DOPEBOY'S PRAYER **II**

By **Eddie "Wolf" Lee**

IF LOVING YOU IS WRONG... **III**

By **Jelissa**

TRUE SAVAGE **VII**

MIDNIGHT CARTEL III

DOPE BOY MAGIC IV

By **Chris Green**

BLAST FOR ME **III**

A SAVAGE DOPEBOY III

CUTTHROAT MAFIA II

By **Ghost**

A HUSTLER'S DECEIT III

KILL ZONE **II**

166

BAE BELONGS TO ME III

A DOPE BOY'S QUEEN II

By **Aryanna**

CHAINED TO THE STREETS III

By **J-Blunt**

KING OF NEW YORK V

COKE KINGS IV

By **T.J. Edwards**

GORILLAZ IN THE BAY V

TEARS OF A GANGSTA II

De'Kari

THE STREETS ARE CALLING II

Duquie Wilson

KINGPIN KILLAZ IV

STREET KINGS III

PAID IN BLOOD III

CARTEL KILLAZ IV

DOPE GODS II

Hood Rich

SINS OF A HUSTLA II

ASAD

TRIGGADALE III

Elijah R. Freeman

KINGZ OF THE GAME V

Playa Ray

SLAUGHTER GANG IV

RUTHLESS HEART IV

T.J. Edwards

By Willie Slaughter

THE HEART OF A SAVAGE III

By Jibril Williams

FUK SHYT II

By Blakk Diamond

THE DOPEMAN'S BODYGAURD II

By Tranay Adams

TRAP GOD II

By Troublesome

YAYO III

A SHOOTER'S AMBITION III

By S. Allen

GHOST MOB

Stilloan Robinson

KINGPIN DREAMS II

By Paper Boi Rari

CREAM

By Yolanda Moore

SON OF A DOPE FIEND II

By Renta

FOREVER GANGSTA II

GLOCKS ON SATIN SHEETS II

By Adrian Dulan

LOYALTY AIN'T PROMISED II

By Keith Williams

THE PRICE YOU PAY FOR LOVE II

DOPE GIRL MAGIC II

By Destiny Skai

TOE TAGZ III

By Ah'Million

CONFESSIONS OF A GANGSTA II

By Nicholas Lock

PAID IN KARMA III

By **Meesha**

I'M NOTHING WITHOUT HIS LOVE II

By Monet Dragun

CAUGHT UP IN THE LIFE II

By Robert Baptiste

NEW TO THE GAME III

By **Malik D. Rice**

LIFE OF A SAVAGE III

By **Romell Tukes**

QUIET MONEY II

By **Trai'Quan**

THE STREETS MADE ME II

By **Larry D. Wright**

THE ULTIMATE SACRIFICE VI

By **Anthony Fields**

THE LIFE OF A HOOD STAR

By Ca$h & Rashia Wilson

Available Now

RESTRAINING ORDER **I & II**

By **CA$H & Coffee**

LOVE KNOWS NO BOUNDARIES **I II & III**

By **Coffee**

RAISED AS A GOON I, II, III & IV

BRED BY THE SLUMS I, II, III

BLAST FOR ME I & II

ROTTEN TO THE CORE I II III

A BRONX TALE I, II, III

DUFFEL BAG CARTEL I II III IV

HEARTLESS GOON I II III IV

A SAVAGE DOPEBOY I II

HEARTLESS GOON I II III

DRUG LORDS I II III

CUTTHROAT MAFIA

By **Ghost**

LAY IT DOWN **I & II**

LAST OF A DYING BREED

BLOOD STAINS OF A SHOTTA I & II III

By **Jamaica**

LOYAL TO THE GAME I II III

LIFE OF SIN I, II III

By **TJ & Jelissa**

BLOODY COMMAS I & II

SKI MASK CARTEL I II & III

KING OF NEW YORK I II,III IV

RISE TO POWER I II III

COKE KINGS I II III

BORN HEARTLESS I II III IV

By **T.J. Edwards**

IF LOVING HIM IS WRONG…I & II

LOVE ME EVEN WHEN IT HURTS I II III

By **Jelissa**

WHEN THE STREETS CLAP BACK I & II III

THE HEART OF A SAVAGE I II

By **Jibril Williams**

A DISTINGUISHED THUG STOLE MY HEART I II & III

LOVE SHOULDN'T HURT I II III IV

RENEGADE BOYS I II III IV

PAID IN KARMA I II

By **Meesha**

A GANGSTER'S CODE I &, II III

A GANGSTER'S SYN I II III

THE SAVAGE LIFE I II III

CHAINED TO THE STREETS I II

By J-Blunt

PUSH IT TO THE LIMIT

By **Bre' Hayes**

BLOOD OF A BOSS **I, II, III, IV, V**

SHADOWS OF THE GAME

By **Askari**

THE STREETS BLEED MURDER **I, II & III**

THE HEART OF A GANGSTA I II& III

T.J. Edwards

By **Jerry Jackson**

CUM FOR ME I II III IV V

An **LDP Erotica Collaboration**

BRIDE OF A HUSTLA **I II & II**

THE FETTI GIRLS **I, II& III**

CORRUPTED BY A GANGSTA I, II III, IV

BLINDED BY HIS LOVE

THE PRICE YOU PAY FOR LOVE

DOPE GIRL MAGIC

By **Destiny Skai**

WHEN A GOOD GIRL GOES BAD

By **Adrienne**

THE COST OF LOYALTY I II III

By Kweli

A GANGSTER'S REVENGE **I II III & IV**

THE BOSS MAN'S DAUGHTERS I II III IV V

A SAVAGE LOVE **I & II**

BAE BELONGS TO ME I II

A HUSTLER'S DECEIT I, II, III

WHAT BAD BITCHES DO I, II, III

SOUL OF A MONSTER I II III

KILL ZONE

A DOPE BOY'S QUEEN

By **Aryanna**

A KINGPIN'S AMBITON

A KINGPIN'S AMBITION **II**

I MURDER FOR THE DOUGH

By **Ambitious**

TRUE SAVAGE I II III IV V VI

DOPE BOY MAGIC I, II, III

MIDNIGHT CARTEL I II

By **Chris Green**

A DOPEBOY'S PRAYER

By **Eddie "Wolf" Lee**

THE KING CARTEL **I, II & III**

By **Frank Gresham**

THESE NIGGAS AIN'T LOYAL **I, II & III**

By **Nikki Tee**

GANGSTA SHYT **I II &III**

By **CATO**

THE ULTIMATE BETRAYAL

By **Phoenix**

BOSS'N UP **I , II & III**

By **Royal Nicole**

I LOVE YOU TO DEATH

By Destiny J

I RIDE FOR MY HITTA

I STILL RIDE FOR MY HITTA

By **Misty Holt**

LOVE & CHASIN' PAPER

By **Qay Crockett**

TO DIE IN VAIN

SINS OF A HUSTLA

By **ASAD**

T.J. Edwards

BROOKLYN HUSTLAZ

By **Boogsy Morina**

BROOKLYN ON LOCK I & II

By **Sonovia**

GANGSTA CITY

By **Teddy Duke**

A DRUG KING AND HIS DIAMOND I & II III

A DOPEMAN'S RICHES

HER MAN, MINE'S TOO I, II

CASH MONEY HO'S

By Nicole Goosby

TRAPHOUSE KING **I II & III**

KINGPIN KILLAZ I II III

STREET KINGS I II

PAID IN BLOOD **I II**

CARTEL KILLAZ I II III

DOPE GODS

By **Hood Rich**

LIPSTICK KILLAH **I, II, III**

CRIME OF PASSION I II & III

By **Mimi**

STEADY MOBBN' **I, II, III**

THE STREETS STAINED MY SOUL

By **Marcellus Allen**

WHO SHOT YA **I, II, III**

SON OF A DOPE FIEND

Renta

GORILLAZ IN THE BAY **I II III IV**

TEARS OF A GANGSTA

DE'KARI

TRIGGADALE I II

Elijah R. Freeman

GOD BLESS THE TRAPPERS I, II, III

THESE SCANDALOUS STREETS I, II, III

FEAR MY GANGSTA I, II, III

THESE STREETS DON'T LOVE NOBODY I, II

BURY ME A G I, II, III, IV, V

A GANGSTA'S EMPIRE I, II, III, IV

THE DOPEMAN'S BODYGAURD

Tranay Adams

THE STREETS ARE CALLING

Duquie Wilson

MARRIED TO A BOSS… I II III

By Destiny Skai & Chris Green

KINGZ OF THE GAME I II III IV

Playa Ray

SLAUGHTER GANG I II III

RUTHLESS HEART I II III

By Willie Slaughter

FUK SHYT

By Blakk Diamond

DON'T F#CK WITH MY HEART I II

By Linnea

ADDICTED TO THE DRAMA I II III

By Jamila

YAYO I II

A SHOOTER'S AMBITION I II

By S. Allen

TRAP GOD

By Troublesome

FOREVER GANGSTA

GLOCKS ON SATIN SHEETS

By Adrian Dulan

TOE TAGZ I II

By Ah'Million

KINGPIN DREAMS

By Paper Boi Rari

CONFESSIONS OF A GANGSTA

By Nicholas Lock

I'M NOTHING WITHOUT HIS LOVE

By Monet Dragun

CAUGHT UP IN THE LIFE

By Robert Baptiste

NEW TO THE GAME I II

By **Malik D. Rice**

Life of a Savage I II

By **Romell Tukes**

LOYALTY AIN'T PROMISED

By **Keith Williams**

Quiet Money

By **Trai'Quan**

THE STREETS MADE ME

By **Larry D. Wright**

THE ULTIMATE SACRIFICE I, II, III, IV, V

KHADIFI

By **Anthony Fields**

THE LIFE OF A HOOD STAR

By Ca\$h & Rashia Wilson

BOOKS BY LDP'S CEO, CA$H

TRUST IN NO MAN

TRUST IN NO MAN 2

TRUST IN NO MAN 3

BONDED BY BLOOD

SHORTY GOT A THUG

THUGS CRY

THUGS CRY 2

THUGS CRY 3

TRUST NO BITCH

TRUST NO BITCH 2

TRUST NO BITCH 3

TIL MY CASKET DROPS

RESTRAINING ORDER

RESTRAINING ORDER 2

IN LOVE WITH A CONVICT

LIFE OF A HOOD STAR

Coming Soon

BONDED BY BLOOD 2

BOW DOWN TO MY GANGSTA

CPSIA information can be obtained
at www.ICGtesting.com
Printed in the USA
LVHW010003150720
660731LV00019B/2290